AMERICAN ABDUCTIONS

A Novel

Mauro Javier Cárdenas

DALKEY ARCHIVE PRESS
Dallas, TX / Rochester, NY

PRAISE FOR MAURO JAVIER CÁRDENAS

APHASIA

"Cárdenas undercuts the idea of a single, stable identity and suggests the self as a many-layered work in progress . . . Original, richly felt, deftly written."
—*Kirkus* (Starred Review)

"*Aphasia* is a novelistic portrait of the internet's ability to help us elide geographical and personal borders. It dramatizes our growing ability to occupy multiple narratives at once — and proves that literature itself can do the same."
—Lily Meyer, *High Country News*

"Mauro Javier Cárdenas's *Aphasia* batters at the limits of guilt, of masculinity, of love and promiscuity, of the American family and English syntax."
—Nicole Krauss, author of *To Be a Man*

"Mauro Javier Cárdenas has knocked down the novel as we know it, and built a cathedral out of the debris. *Aphasia* is monumental, funny, potent, and fresh. It marks a new beginning."
—Carlos Fonseca, author of *Austral* and *Natural History*

"Brainy and decadent, playful and outrageous, *Aphasia* marks the comeback of the Self in a spiraling trip into contemporary manhood and the Latin American spirit that will render you speechless."
—Pola Oloixarac, author of *Mona*

PRAISE FOR MAURO JAVIER CÁRDENAS

THE REVOLUTIONARIES TRY AGAIN

"This is an original, insubordinate novel, like his grammar, like his syntax, but fabulously, compellingly readable."
—Valerie Miles, *New York Times Book Review*

"This is a book at once haunting and haunted, rippling with the ghosts of Latin America's atrocities, disappointments, colonial strangleholds, insurgencies and fierce hopes, a book at once specific to Ecuador's historical realities and bursting with significance to our whole hemisphere."
—Carolina De Robertis, *San Francisco Chronicle*

"[A] high-octane, high-modernist debut novel from the gifted, fleet Mauro Javier Cardenas."
—Harper's

"An amazing book rife with intelligence and love for the potential of one's homeland."
—Electric Literature

"The political action tends to take place on the periphery as Cardenas dizzyingly leaps from character to character, from street protests to swanky soirees, and from lengthy uninterrupted interior monologues to rapid-fire dialogues and freewheeling satirical radio programs, resulting in extended passages of brilliance."
—*Publishers Weekly* (starred review)

Deep Vellum | Dalkey Archive Press
3000 Commerce Street
Dallas, Texas 75226

dalkeyarchive.com

First North American Edition, 2024

Support for this publication has been provided in part by grants from the National Endowment for the Arts, the Texas Commission on the Arts, the City of Dallas Office of Arts and Culture, the Communities Foundation of Texas, and the Addy Foundation.

Paperback ISBN: 9781628975185
Ebook ISBN: 9781628975437
Library of Congress Control Number: 2024934019

Cover design by Jack Smyth
Interior design by Anuj Mathur

Printed in Canada

AMERICAN ABDUCTIONS

A Novel

Part I

Ada's Father

Take him, Ada wrote almost ten years ago, when she was still a senior in high school and Mr. Poland, her English teacher, had tried to teach her and her retrograde classmates how to craft compelling opening sentences for their college admissions essays, emphasizing the word craft as if the components at their disposal weren't words in English but crayons and glitter and whatever else preschool children are given to pass the time before they die — now children, Doctor Sueño says, today we're going to craft Noah's ark — can we stack it with seals? — ark ark ark — today we'll focus on crafting compelling opening sentences, Mr. Poland said in that placid voice of his that reminded Ada of those ridiculous people who try to console mourners at funerals — leave them alone, Mr. Poland — Mr. Poland I'm from Poland, a classmate of hers had often repeated as if it were the funniest joke, and I did laugh almost every time, Ada says, that squalid girl from El Salvador claiming she was from Poland, take him, Ada wrote since she'd chosen her father's abduction as the subject of her college admissions essay and yet she crossed out her words because she knew she shouldn't have written them based on a number of reasons that were probably not clear to her then but that she has been able to consider in the last ten years, especially in the last five since she has had to drive to and from work, an hour each way, Ada the architect driving back to her apartment from her architect's office as she's doing now, what a joke, although during these long drives she's tried to distract herself from the unpleasant past by listening to lectures on metaphysics, pataphysics, Polish poetry, dreams, her favorite lectures not lectures but oneiric monologues by Doctor Sueño, Doctor Sueño I'm from Sueño, Ada says to the windshield, to the road, to the sun coming down, unconcerned others might think she's talking to herself because they'll probably think she's giving instructions to Leonora, her car, take him, Ada wrote, and the reasons, according to her, that she crossed out her words were that (1) if she wrote them down they might reactivate an irreversible proceeding against her father that would have otherwise remained dormant — I'm not superstitious, Ada would reply if someone asked her, but if you write down, for instance, I would like to die and return as a buzzard, and you read that out loud every day, wouldn't that alter the course of your life? — don't ever let your mind near a palm reader because if she says to you I see Poland in your future, Ada says, even if you don't believe in palm reading because, say, you have no palms — ark ark ark — the idea that Poland's in your future might be enough to alter the course of your life even if you don't end up ever flying to Poland, do you understand? — one day I will fly to Poland and picnic at the Zydowski cemetery and cry like an eagle — they used to pour millet on graves or poppy seeds to feed the dead who would come disguised as birds, Milosz says, I put this book here for you, who once lived, so that you should visit us no more — cry like an eagle, her father used to sing whenever something was amiss at home — my father had a knack for singing songs that contained words my sister and I had just said — oh no a B+ in math I'm going to cry — cry like an eagle / to the sea — quit it, Tata — not the course of your life that's too melodramatic, Ada thinks, the course of the subpathways of your life, which she imagines as the pathways across the Zydowski cemetery in Warsaw as seen from above, (2) if placid Poland asked her to read her opening sentence out loud, he would have had to strain himself to remain placid and polite and say very good, Ada, quite compelling, but she didn't want him to strain for her, although sometimes over the years when she returns to Mr. Poland's classroom in her mind she thinks why not have him strain for me for a change, eh?, (3) if placid Poland asked her to read her opening sentence out loud, her classmates would assume it was autobiographical and pity her, poor Ada still stuck in that moment when the American abductors captured her father as he was driving her and her sister to school, which she recorded on her phone when she was thirteen years old, a moment everyone in her classroom had probably already watched online, yes but she's not going to think about that now so she says to Leonora shuffle and play please and Doctor Sueño says hypnagogic hallucinations, not now doctor, Ada says, a universe comprised of exceptions implies an equivalence between imaginary solutions, an Alfred Jarry impersonator says, nope, out with you, Ada says, dear humans I grew up with a family of roly polies, Ada's father says, my parents left me to fight in the anteater war and never came back, shuffle and skip, Ada says, you have a father and he likes cheese, Doctor Sueño says, that's physics, if you have a father, he likes cheese, that's metaphysics, you don't have a father and he likes cheese, that's pataphysics and you, Ada, but my father didn't like cheese as much as squid ceviche, lomo saltado, words that lose their resonance in translation — say urraca in English — magpie — see? — (4) everyone would think she was so mean — I am so mean so what? — (5) everyone would think she was inadvertently confessing a shameful family secret, of which there was none — a family without shameful secrets isn't a family, Ada — (6) Mr. Poland would detain her after class and send her to the placid principal, who would send her to the placid psychologist, who would send her to the placid psychiatrist, who would regale her with a rendition of Schumann's Traumerei and mouth the words trauma, post trauma, disorderly trauma, and so on — do I have the Harry Trauman, ma'am? — huh? — and yes, you can still find her video and the variations on her video online — want to watch Ada sob like the sea? click here now! — and what she remembers more than her video of the abductors capturing her father while he was driving her and her sister to school is the asinine interviews she had to give to try to save him — yes I miss my father — yes I want him back — sob to the nth power is that enough? — the reassuring slogans that were expected of her — we are stronger than the Racist in Chief — I have to be strong for my dad — and so on, as if someone had pressed the deportation button on the American narrative machine and a whole cast of characters had come alive, including Esteban Ramos from Univision, who thought it would be a fantastic idea to replicate on camera our drive to the location where the abductors had captured my father and ask me how does it feel to return to the scene — bad? — yes that's it! — we could feel the weight of what had transpired, Esteban Ramos says in a video you can still find online, so we quickly decided to leave — every location can be negated by an imaginary opposite location, Doctor Sueño says, do you understand? — what is the opposite of Monterey Boulevard and Edna Street? — a location that, according to the official manual for American abductions, was considered sensitive because it was a half a mile from a school, my school — sensitive locations should generally be avoided, the manual says, and require prior approval from an appropriate supervisory official — and so in an agency building someone had to call or message a supervisory official who called or messaged his supervisory official who was probably on vacation in Cancun or Cabo please hold for a week / ten days eventually a supervisory official chancing upon the memo entitled Antonio José Rodriguez Deportation Proceedings, and perhaps because the name reminded the supervisory official of some kid in high school who had outpaced him at soccer and / or mathematics, he stamped it and said out with him, and later, after her father had been captured and hundreds of thousands of people around the world were watching her video of her father asking what have I done, officer, the supervisory official probably watched it too and left an anonymous comment below it that said ice / ice baby great job ICE, illegal is illegal and wrong is wrong bye you forgot the crybaby in the backseat, for years Ada arguing in her mind with the thousands of messages berating her and her father, even after she discovered some of the comments had been manufactured by bots controlled by a Pale American in Salt Lake City — twelve million to go please continue to remove the illegal alien infestation — except the comments by Doctor Sueño, of course, which made no sense to anyone but her, just as it made no sense to anyone but her to feel, for no more than a few seconds, proud that the supervisory official of the supervisory official of the supervisory official in an agency building had taken time out of his busy schedule to focus on her father — if enough time passes, Doctor Sueño says, even the most preposterous possibilities will navigate the sea of your mind — cry like an eagle / to the sea — just as it made no sense to anyone but her to laugh at some of the videos her video had spawned for instance the video of her video but with sappy music instead of her sister politely asking the abductors where were they taking her father, as if someone figured hey no one's going to feel sorry enough for you people let me add sad violin music to the video of your father saying I've done nothing wrong, officer, or how about the video from a self proclaimed irreverent news organization from China that, via computer animation as if from an obsolete video game, replicated the trajectory from her house to the sensitive location as if it were a car chase, the abductors rushing to drag her father out of the car as if it were a drug bust, the video game representation of Ada recording her father's capture with her phone from the backseat of the car, waterfalls of tears surging from her eyes, no not waterfalls, more like someone's comical representation of lawn sprinklers superimposed on the eyes of the video game representation of me, or how about the video by Doctor Sueño that had removed the original images of three abductors handcuffing her father and taking him away from her in a black unmarked sedan with tinted windows so no one in those placid neighborhoods of San Francisco would be disturbed by the images of her father shackled on his way to a detention center, the video by Doctor Sueño that was just images of American skyscrapers as seen from above combined with the audio from her original video, the sound of her sobbing for the whole two minutes and fourteen seconds she'd held her phone to record her father's capture — listen to this video every night before going to sleep, Doctor Sueño says, and I guarantee you placid dreams — let the sounds of Ada's sobbing soothe you, Doctor Sueño says, let your mind wander to far away galaxies, etc. — but if you zoom above the Zydowski cemetery on a map online, Ada thinks, as she had done one evening five or three or however many years ago, soon after listening to Edward Hirsch's lecture on Polish poetry while driving to work (one evening at Old St. Mary's Cathedral she heard Edward Hirsch read about a black rhinoceros at the Brookfield Zoo that reminded him of his uncle's extended family — what does it feel like to have two horns, Edward Hirsch said, tilting up on a huge head? — and afterward, when only two or three lanky poets and a widow remained in that church, she approached him and held his hands, this poet with a Chicago accent who had the benevolent look of someone she hopes to see on her deathbed, and said to him they've taken my father, and he understood — no, Ada, you didn't approach him, didn't hold his hands, didn't plead with him, you watched him from afar and afterward you read his poems out loud in your kitchen), you can't see the real pathways through the Zydowski cemetery on the online maps but green bushes with dotted lines superimposed by some software engineer — there must be a grid here, the software engineer probably said to his cat, otherwise how else to know where the dead people are? — miauczec? — and as Ada drives back to her apartment in El Cerrito, believing for no discernable reason that once she arrives at her apartment her sister will finally pick up her phone, she asks Leonora to call her sister again (her sister who had been in the front seat when the abductors captured her father, who had attended the rallies before and after her father was deported back to Bogotá even though he was an American citizen with no criminal record, her sister who soon after graduating from Yale, as her father had done before her, sold all her belongings and said to hell with this Racist American country and flew back to be with our dad — why didn't you, Ada? — I waited too long I thought I wanted my own life here we're here to stay and then everyone was saying that the latest replica of the Racist in Chief that the Pale Americans had elected was ordering the borders shut in both directions for all Latin Americans and the descendants of all Latin Americans for the good of the nation I'm so sorry — her sister who had called her today, early in the morning while Ada was in a meeting about Escher bathrooms in office buildings and left a message saying Dad had a heart attack he's not going to, I don't know how long he'll, call me please, and as Leonora continues to ring her sister, an enforcement patrol approaches her on the Bay Bridge, staying level with her, and as the man on the passenger side assesses her with what looks like a periscope on his hand and apparently clears her because the patrol car is speeding away, and as her sister in Bogotá continues to not answer her phone, and as Doctor Sueño says teleport the contents of your mind by holding still — where was I? — ah, yes, she's glad she purchased the black market window tincture programmed to pale her skin, a window tincture with an input network that accounts for meteorological conditions like too much sun, for instance, which might otherwise pale her into looking like a ghost — bad ghosts are our removal priority number two thank you for asking — a window tincture that wouldn't have helped my father ten years ago, Ada says, take him, Ada wrote, Mr. Poland I'm from Poland, that squalid girl from El Salvador said, and perhaps I found her refrain funny because I associated Poland with potatoes, Ada says, with pale plump Polish people eating bowls of potatoes whereas Avelica from El Salvador looked as if she hadn't eaten in weeks — I've never been separated from him before, Ada said at a rally in front of hundreds of Latin Americans who would soon be deported, too — sana / sana / culito de rana — don't cry we have to be strong, her sister said and still says in Ada's video of her father's capture — not in my version, Doctor Sueño says — learn to cry in English ha ha — take him, Ada said after Mr. Poland asked her to read her opening statement out loud, activating options (2) (3) (6), yes but before these options were activated I was at home placing blueberries on my waffles in a kitchen wallpapered with my childhood paintings — please photograph each of your paintings for me, her father had messaged her from Bogotá, or even better invent a few new ones for me? — here's a drawing of me smiling next to the word Lilttutobpg, Ada wrote, which obviously means I don't have horns — you lumber around in your skin of armor, Edward Hirsh said, like an exiled general or a grounded unicorn — and nothing memorable happened during breakfast and nothing memorable was said on our way to school before we heard the sirens, although of course I've imagined and reimagined memorable words that might have altered the outcome — a stomach ache due to too many waffles we have to stay home, Tata — a rhinoceros has escaped from the zoo we have to stay home, Tata — at first we heard the sirens behind us and we thought oh no the police, Ada says, we thought an ambulance has materialized to take my father away before the abductors can capture him, what have I done, officer, my father said, shut up we have a removal order for you, the whatever you want to call that individual said, don't cry we have to be strong, her sister said, we're going to take him here's the phone number give us a couple of hours we still need to process him, that piece of shit said, take him, Ada said after Mr. Poland asked her to read her opening sentence out loud, who needs a father anyway?

Interpretations

A rosary equals a Radisson Hotel, Doctor Sueño says, a Radisson Hotel equals the Walt Disney concert hall in Los Angeles, same tapestry on the carpets, seats, passageways to the secret sleep rooms, as if a committee of decorators, let's call them that, a committee of decorators instead of a committee of curators of the wallpapers of transience, as if a committee of decorators surveyed the constituents of classical music at their retirement homes and discovered the constituents of classical music used to vacation at Radisson Hotels around the world, and by the world I mean Cabo San Lucas — the Radisson reward points in Cabo are just unbelievable, doctor — and so the committee of decorators, not to be confused with the committee of gladiators who wear Christ sandals and shave their legs and gather on Mondays after their office jobs to talk about creatine and lasers, decorated the Walt Disney concert hall like a Radisson Hotel, and so when you and your father entered that concert hall for a performance of Arvo Pärt's Symphony No. 4 and your father said this concert hall looks like a Radisson Hotel, you said can I please have that Coca-Cola you promised me already, and later, across time and space and whatever else elicits images of intergalactic journeys, you, instead of linking your father's childhood with the rosary hanging from the rearview mirror of your father's car, a rosary that millions of people might have seen in passing when you, from the backseat of your father's car, pointed your phone's video camera in the direction of the windshield, which was the same direction where three American abductors wearing fake police vests could be seen handcuffing your father, you, instead of linking that rosary with your father's childhood, his days at San Luis Gonzaga High School in Bogotá, when he'd wanted to become a Jesuit priest, as he'd written in his first novel, which was later banned in the United States and its allied countries since your father fell under the unsavory category of Latin American, linked that rosary with a Radisson Hotel, in other words with the Walt Disney Music Hall, where, on the stage, an Estonian tolled an ancient bell, the kind you find as ornaments at cathedrals — this bell belonged to Barabbas, ladies and gentlemen — and yet others linked your father's rosary with you, Ada, some of whom, having nothing else to do with the fruits of their religious lives — we ran out of reward points, doctor — founded online prayer groups like El Rosario de Ada (ERDA) and A Rosary for Ada (ARFA) — last night I closed my eyes, a member of ERDA posted, and instead of praying for Ada I recited from memory passages from the fictions of Amparo Dávila, last night I closed my eyes, a member of ARFA posted, and instead of praying for Ada I tried to reimagine Ada's video, frame by frame, every morning before I make breakfast for my cat, a member of ERDA posted, I watch Ada's video instead of praying for her because who am I going to pray to, and yes, I know, watching her video every morning is as useless as praying, but perhaps one day, after thousands of mornings watching her video, I will at last burst out of grief and this minute explosion will overturn something, but who will take care of your cat, another member of ERDA posted, tell us your name and your recurrent dream, Doctor Sueño says, my name is Roberto and my dream's name is Ocean, Roberto says, cleverness does pass the time, Doctor Sueño says, I am by the sea and I drown, Roberto says, I am by the sea, the edge of the sea, watching the tranquility of the sea, and I as near the sea a giant wave appears and overtakes me and I drown and so I think in my other life I must have drown in the sea, are other lives allowed, someone says, please no questions or interjections while the session's taking place, Doctor Sueño says, my name's Jonas and I am a conscientious interjector, Jonas says, go back inside the whale and shut up, someone else says, any questions or interjections, Doctor Sueño says, even an errant word might lead us astray to faraway galaxies, that doesn't sound so bad, Jonas says, not at all sure let's voyage as far away as possible, Doctor Sueño says, but not during Roberto's dream session now Roberto, thank you for calling in and thank you for allowing us to transmit your session live, oh no you're recording me, I wouldn't dream of it ha ha, Roberto says, jokes do pass the time, Doctor Sueño says, if anyone needs to exhaust their whale associations do it now, Jonas says, I wish I could quote from Moby-Dick do we have time for a quick search online, someone says, I am sitting in a room, Ada's father says, different than the one you're in now, everything in your dreams is you, Roberto, Doctor Sueño says, become the waves, the little ones and the giant ones, I am a giant wave, Roberto says, I am very destructive, no one can fight me, I can destroy everything, kill anyone, please repeat for us the part about the giant wave, Doctor

Sueño says, Leonora turn up the volume of Doctor Sueño's transmission, Ada says, I am very destructive, Roberto says, I can kill, what comes into your mind when you say you are destructive you can kill, Doctor Sueño says, when I am upset what happens to me is I can't control myself I want to launch myself at others attack them, Roberto says, has that happened to you before, Doctor Sueño says, yes I've become so upset I've done things I shouldn't have done, Roberto says, you are the sand, Doctor Sueño says, I am the sand and I am very soft but the waves come and they take me away, Roberto says, I am a little wave I don't ripple anything, Ada says as she drives past Treasure Island on the Bay Bridge, sure she will dream of the sea tonight, I am a giant wave I can destroy everything I can kill, Roberto says, but I haven't always been this way sometimes I am soft, have you killed anyone, Doctor Sueño says, no, Roberto says, in that case let's replace the word kill with the word hurt have you hurt anyone, Doctor Sueño says, yes, Roberto says, I can hurt I can destroy I am very upset, what are you upset about, Doctor Sueño says, I don't know about how do I get rid of this giant wave that keeps following me, Roberto says, I'm going to say a word, Doctor Sueño says, and you will tell me what comes to mind, urraca, Ada says, hunger, Doctor Sueño says, churrasco, Roberto says, mnemocartography, Ada says, pencil, Doctor Sueño says, pen, Roberto says, sad, Doctor Sueño says, very sad, Roberto says, family, Doctor Sueño says, swamp, Roberto says, home, Doctor Sueño says, when I was twelve years old faceless guards took my father away they kicked him until his sprawled body on the floor halted its movements I grew up with an uncle here in Bogotá but he had to work so I remained at home, alone, Roberto says, and I was very scared, and I learned to always be upset so others would be scared of me so no one would come close to me and hurt me, I am a giant wave, Ada says, you are a giant wave, Doctor Sueño says, I can climb mountains, Ada says, toll bells, if you try to escape them you might end up on a boat, Jonas doesn't say, and people on the boat will throw you overboard and you will end up inside a fish, except no one will imagine you bursting out of the fish, yes but the problem is no one bursts out of grief, Ada says, grief is like Mozart hearing the entirety of his requiem at the same time, all the time, like stepping out of your car while you're driving and hoping for a swift outcome except that would require enough energy to open the door, unbuckle the seatbelt, tilt outward, and so on, I will lock the doors if you unbuckle your seatbelt while we're in motion, Leonora says as the doors lock and unlock and lock, so we're stuck together for a while should I transmit your father reading your roly poly story for us?

Case Study

The math can't be that difficult, Antonio thinks, because he's not trying to estimate the exact day or week the American abductors will come for him, which maybe he could approximate with a discrete time to event logistic model, also known as a survival model, although to build a decent survival model he would need a stratified random sample of deportation eligible individuals in the United States, and this sample of individuals would need to come with a 1 / 0 indicator for those deported and those not yet deported, also known as the target variable, along with explanatory variables like ethnicity, immigration status, income, proximity to an immigration detention center, etc., but no, he isn't focused on the exact day or week but the approximate year the abductors will come for him so he can prepare his bank accounts and his paltry stock options from his fifteen years at Prudential Investments as a senior data analyst so that his former wife can immediately change the access codes when the abductors come for him because there are already reports circulating that, just as during previous waves of abductions and deportations in previous eras of world history, the abductors had a way of coercing their detainees into handing over necklaces, bracelets, watches, or in the case of this era, the American abductors are coercing their detainees into handing over access codes — if you tell me how to access your bank accounts I will make sure they give you a fair hearing — no — I'll even put in a good word for you — no — hand them over or we'll also detain your wife and kids — 6666 — and once his former wife changes his access codes she can take over his accounts and provide for their daughters, Ada and Eva, who are eleven and eight years old still, not that he's been able to save that much but enough for the quantity to feel like a thoughtful college graduation gift — all those years at Prudential Investments our father wasn't just running SQL queries and building hidden Markov models but thinking of us, Ada — and here Antonio likes to imagine his daughters outside Yale's University Church, holding a vase labelled Tata's Money Tree — your vase needs to lose some weight, Eva — oh we'll take care of that ha ha — Yale's University Church, where, on a first date with a harpist who was also a rugby player, he'd heard Mozart's Requiem for the first time, almost twenty five years ago, in any case the estimation of the approximate year the American abductors will come for him can leverage less precise quantitative methods, or rather no method other than a series of reasonable assumptions, the kind that showcases your business acumen during case study interviews like the ones he underwent so many years ago, when he was about to graduate from Yale and didn't know what to do with his life so he tried to be what everyone else with an economics degree was trying to be, a management consultant or an investment banker, what are you doing, Ada says, quantifying when the dinosaurs will return what are you doing,

Antonio says, dinner is ready mama says come now or eat chicken forever, Ada says, carry me there, Eva says, I am Eva's aging transportation system, Antonio says, how was your day, Antonio's former wife says, other than being stopped by a policeman on the street yet again, Antonio says, why, Ada says, how, Eva says, would you like me to tell it to you dramatically, melodramatically, or obliquely, Antonio says, dramatically, Ada says, okay, Antonio says, so, I was falling asleep at work and didn't want to dream of dinosaurs because everyone knows that if you dream of dinosaurs you snore too loud and I didn't want to wake up my coworkers so I shut down my cubicle, what's a cubicle, Eva says, it's when an ice cube and a popsicle get married, Ada says, and so I shut down the product of a sticky melting marriage and ambled to the street, searching for a cappuccino, when for no reason whatsoever, unless picking your nose counts as an offense, ewww, Eva says, a policeman accosted me and asked to see my identification, maybe he knew about your dinosaur smuggling business, Ada says, okay now melodramatically, Eva says, I couldn't take it anymore my eyes were closing against my will I needed coffee beans grinded into a cup even though the price of coffee is impossible these days and my back hurts, Antonio says, sana sana / culito de rana, Antonio's former wife says, and then, Antonio says, as if Satan had aimed a spotlight at me, an angry policeman chased me and I said I don't deserve this I wasn't doing anything why are you here he shouted as I ran away from him, okay now obliquely, Ada says, due to circumstances I have mostly forgotten I wasn't able to enjoy my coffee today, Antonio says, dishes on the sink please, Antonio's former wife says, who wants to play checkers with me, Antonio says, but neither Ada nor Eva want to play with him because they want to finish reading the novels in their Dream Trilogy Series instead, one quick game of Uno, Antonio says, tomorrow, Tata, Eva says, who taught these children how to overread, Antonio's former wife says, fine, Antonio says, and so Antonio returns to his case study, which can't be that difficult, good afternoon, thank you for having me and thank you for sharing this stimulating case study, to estimate my deportation year I will need to make some general assumptions, first, that the current 12 million undocumented immigrants remains constant as our starting point, second, that the rate of growth of immigration agents also remains constant at 400%, third, that I will not increase the probability of being captured by writing about the horror of deportations, fourth, let's assume, based on some data I researched online this week, not because I am a naturalized citizen from Colombia at risk of deportation, no, but purely out of inquisitiveness, that the rate of capture per agent also remains constant at 2 immigrants per day, so that's 10 undocumented immigrants per week times 52 weeks equals 520 undocumented immigrants per agent per year, so the numerator is 12 million undocumented immigrants, and the denominator is 520 undocumented immigrants per agent per year times 5,800 current enforcement agents equals roughly 3 million, so 12 million divided by 3 million is four years to capture everyone who's undocumented, now, before you celebrate these numbers let me clarify that I think the capture rate per day has been overestimated, but for our purposes it provides us with a useful range, if capture rate = 1 per day, then we double the number of years to capture everyone to 6, if capture rate = 0.5 per day, then 12, so anywhere between 3 and 12 years to capture everyone, which can be calibrated as we receive more data, now I see the three of you are frowning, and yes, I agree, I have not answered your question yet because I am documented and I should have mentioned at the beginning that I am assuming a linear progression with immigration enforcement focused on persecuting the undocumented first, then persecuting permanent resident aliens next, the ones who aren't as pale as yourself, of course, but that goes without saying, then persecuting naturalized citizens like myself, which, I know, I know, is too simplistic of an assumption because once the undocumented get wind of the increase in deportations, they will stop taking their kids to school, they will stop driving to the grocery store, etc., and so the rate of capture per day is likely to decrease as deportations increase unless laws are passed that allow agents to stop anyone who doesn't look as pale as yourself, and so yes, you are correct, to keep up an upward trend of deportations, which is likely to be their measure of success, the immigration enforcement agency is likely to forfeit linear progression in their removal prioritization and mandate that all non-Pale Americans will be deported in no particular order, very good, Robert Half says, but we can't hire anyone who uses words like persecuting, my apologies I should have said assailing, Antonio says, the enforcers are just doing their jobs, John Guane says, you are correct I should have said an increase in productivity as a function of new laws assailing everyone but you, Antonio says, we also want to warn you we just called the immigration enforcement hotline, Ronald Watt says, and they're coming for you now, Robert Half says, stay in your seat and don't make a scene, John Guane says, this is the worst interview ever, Antonio says, can I at least finish my mortadella sandwich?

Eva's Father

I am the prodigal son, Eva thinks in the waiting room of the Hospital Luis Vernaza, I am, according to aunt Estela, who no longer thinks Brad Pitt conspired to deport her, biblical, whereas you missed your cue and never came back, Ada, and yet according to our father, my father, who used to favor you when we were little because you were better at pretending you enjoyed those atonal recitals at the Center for New Music — a concert hall with unfamiliar progressions is fertile space for interplanetary associations, Eva's father wrote — you are the prodigal son, in other words he still believes you might come back, even though sometimes, after his morning writing sessions yield nothing of interest yet again, he pontificates — you wouldn't know how he pontificates because you aren't here, Ada — about how he always wanted you and I to have our own lives, implying, without meaning to, although not meaning to isn't an excuse to mean to, that I was weak or at fault for not having my own life, for leaving my own so-called life in that racist American country to be with him in Colombia, a country that is just as racist, incidentally, as if something might be amiss with me for linking my own life with his — I am sorry I didn't mean it that way, Eva — yes you did — I don't appreciate your comments about Ada and I having our own lives, Eva said to her father too many years ago, plus we're prodigal daughters not prodigal sons, plus you mistake my wish to be near you with subjugation, as if I couldn't exist without you or only existed to think of you, what is Tata thinking about is precisely what I don't think every morning when I wake up, just as I didn't think of you every morning when I was growing up with you and Mama in San Francisco, when I would wake up in phases, as if inside a tunnel, like your multicolor tunnel from your Hypnagogia installation, Eva's father said, yes except in that installation I renamed the phases modules and invented instructions to replicate my languid trajectory away from sleep, Eva said, hyperventilate yourself and transport whatever you hallucinate to the next module, Eva's father said, so yes I would awake in modules, Eva said, the memory of the evening's dreams mixing with the sounds of you and Mama goofing around in the kitchen, knowing you were hugging Mama too tightly because Perrito would bark at you whenever you did, merge your hallucination with the first creature that comes to mind and carry it to the next module, Eva's father said, knowing Ada was already awake and dressed and reading her Egyptian adventure stories in the living room, Eva said, knowing Mama was about to come in and wake me up, and I would pretend I was asleep so she would come in and sit on the edge of the bed and tell me daylight had arrived and was waiting for me, as if daylight was a person, as if daylight was a talking sunflower carrying a briefcase, which is how I often imagined daylight for who knows what reason, and yes, sometimes upon awakening I would wonder if you were still home, Tata, if you hadn't yet gone to write your fictions at Prudential Investments — I'm a sophisticated writer I can't wash the dishes today — give him the sophisticated sponge, Mama — and sometimes, in the morning, when you hadn't yet gone to write your fictions, I would tell you my dreams — I wrote down many of your dreams, Eva's father said — I read 165 words in my dream last night I counted them, Tata — and sometimes you read to us the stories of Leonora Carrington before going to bed — the one about the face eating hyena, remember? — and our father, my father, an octopus of tubes in this backward hospital, shut his Encyclopedia of Monstrous Architecture in our living room here in Bogotá, as if I was still five years old and this was the nth time I was interrupting him with questions about crocodiles or dental floss and fine what is it, Evarista, smiling at me so as to let me know his melodrama of interruption was an act, but instead of joking about what I'd said about what he'd said about having our own lives or making a skit out of it as he always did when we were growing up — make me a sandwich, Tata — your sandwich will be ready in five. minutes.and [pause] twenty.seconds: to hear this message again press 1, to have your father exit your room press 2, to hear him sing a song press 3 — two! — that's all folks! [exit father] — you are right and I am sorry, Eva, Eva's father said, what am I right about, Eva said, when I left Bogotá for the first time, Eva's father said, when I was seventeen or eighteen years old, I was glad I was never going to see my father again, and I never saw my father again, and so to me having my own life always meant having a life away from my father, and on top of that I always imagined that in old age I would end up alone, passing the time before the end of this life / farce in a puny office space in a forsaken building, which is how my father ended up, or at least that's the last living space I remember him living in — installation idea, Eva writes in the waiting room of the Hospital Luis Vernaza, a piece for one person / a questionnaire sent months in advance please fill out an inventory of your father's belongings include a favorite photo of your father / the instructions are as follows you enter a bare office space with your father's belongings arranged as if in an abandoned storage space / except there's a mattress where an actor dressed as your father is sleeping your father won't wake up as long as you're there as you exit you will hear him shuffling around / research algorithm to determine how to arrange belongings in office space — and so it is amazing to me that you are here, Eva, Eva's father said, it's like I am living in the right parallel life, the one I am probably pining for from the wrong parallel life, where I should have ended up but didn't, and in that wrong parallel life I am looking back at the time you were born and regretting leaving you and your sister and your mother, as I had tried to do in the right parallel life, why are you telling me this now, Eva said, I had a prophetic dream about death by crocodiles, Eva's father said, why did you want to leave us, Eva said, would you like to sit down, Eva's father said, I don't want to sit down but I will sit down anyway, Eva said, I was too young, Eva's father said, never wanted children, or rather I had never imagined wanting children, you met somebody, Eva said, that too yes, Eva's father said, a writer, Eva said, I used to read her science fiction stories to you that was twenty years ago, Eva's father said, I don't remember, Eva said, the one written in the form of a Q&A with the chatbot of a detective agency called Parallel Longings, which clients hire to investigate what happens in their parallel lives, Eva's father said, what ever happened to her, Eva said, she married an American charlatan who doesn't read, Eva's father said, rarely published anything else of significance, was deported to South Korea, lost her reason, The End, you regret it, Eva said, I don't and I do, Eva's father said, imagine having multiple parallel lives, and I don't mean this in a science fiction way but in an imagination way, as in our imagination, and this is just a hypothesis, of course, might have the capacity to unspool multiple possible lives so that when I decided to stay with you instead of leaving you for her, for instance, let's call this life Eva(+), my imagination continued to unspool my life with her so that that life, let's call that one Eva(-), exists somewhere in my memory, from beginning to end, even if it didn't happen, somewhere near the Kunst Werke Institute for Contemporary Art the science fiction writer and my father are reading Leonora Carrington to each other, Eva said, somewhere in Manhattan the science fiction writer and I are ending our relationship while somewhere in Madrid you are living with your mother and your new father, Eva's father said, and in Eva(-) I regret leaving you most of the time, whereas in Eva(+) I don't regret leaving you most of the time and do regret leaving her almost none of the time, and so regretting and not regretting can coexist except in the regret narratives we tell others because most of us prefer the fantasy of one or the other, why did you tell me both, Eva said, because you are old enough now and perhaps this coexistence of regrets can be a seed for one of your installations, Eva's father said, I came here for you and not for you, Eva said, exactly, Eva's father said, and perhaps one day you will tell me about your parallel life in which you didn't come here and I will tell you my parallel life in which you didn't come here, Eva(+)(-), Eva said — shouldn't you be calling your sister to let her know about my heart attack? — should I tell it to her dramatically, melodramatically, or obliquely? — you know my preferences, Evarista — due to unforeseen circumstances our father will no longer be able to communicate with you — everything remains the same in our family except for one heart shaped engine that's kaput now — we no longer have to mar our memory of father with real time data of father — oh that's a good one — are you Antonio Rodriguez's espouse, the doctor at the Hospital Luis Vernaza says, he doesn't have a espouse he has a daughter, Eva says, are you Antonio's Rodriguez's daughter, the doctor says, yes what's the, Eva says, thank you for your life near mine, Eva, Eva's father said, he's stable, the doctor says, I don't think he would agree with that assessment, Eva says, your unstable father is stable for now does that work, the doctor says, much better is this the part I say is he going to make it doctor and you say make what and I say clay crocodiles and mud men benosed with carrots, Eva says, I think you might want to go in and say goodbye, the doctor says, you just told me he's stable, Eva says, I'm sorry I get nervous I don't like giving people bad news we've stabilized him for now, the doctor says, I have a list here of my father's requirements in case of impending death and saying goodbye melodramatically isn't on the list, Eva says, you don't have to read it to me if you don't, the doctor says, dear daughter, Eva reads, it has come to my attention that I am dying and therefore the time has come to activate the following activities: one, pudding, just kidding I hate pudding, two, wait, no, one, stream Drumming by Steve Reich (did I ever tell you that when my grandfather Enrique was dying in a hospital bed in Gainesville, Florida, my mother brought two tiny portable speakers and placed them around his head and, claiming grandpa loved New Age music, which wasn't true, streamed New Age music straight to his head can you imagine listening to someone's saccharine idea of the ethereal on your deathbed?), two, stream Cuando Vuelva a Tu Lado by Edye Gormé y Los Panchos, three, read out loud the Cesar Bruto epigraph of Hopscotch by Julio Cortázar in Spanish, which I have included here for you, I have to attend to other matters but I, the doctor says, four, tell the doctor not to look at you pityingly as he's doing now, Eva says, I'm sorry do you need tissues, the doctor says, tell him to grow a cactus and sit on it, Antonio says, yes thank you I don't want to get these eye droppings on his requirements, Eva says, I'll be back I'll take you to his room in a few minutes, the doctor says, siempre que viene el tiempo fresco, Eva reads to herself, o sea al medio del otonio, a mí me da la loca de pensar ideas de tipo eséntrico y esótico, como ser por egenplo que me gustaría venirme golondrina para agarrar y volar a los paíx adonde haiga calor, o ser hormiga para meterme bien adentro de una curva y comer los productos guardados en el verano o de ser una víbora como las del solojicO, and here Eva pauses and wonders if perhaps this epigraph, her father's last written message to her, contains a hidden message that will only become apparent to her after he dies — if you read it in front of a mirror upside down Julio Cortázar will appear and exclaim joven! — Berthe Trépat at your service — although she knows she will interpret anything her father has written as a hidden message to her after he dies, quit it with the hidden messages, her father would say, and focus instead on how this epigraph contains everything that's worthwhile about literature: (1) the ridiculous language with the misspelled words that negate their own meaning, as if someone was trying to paint his bathroom but the paint kept leaping to the floor and cracking jokes about your horrible brushstroke technique — pinche pintor! — (2) the metamorphosis from human to swallow, rising toward the sky not like a swallow but as a swallow because he has become a swallow, crawling free as an ant and later as a not so free snake in the zoo, (3) the unexpected transformation from being a warm snake in the zoo back to being a human who's lamenting about the condition of other humans who are cold because they can't afford to buy clothes, (4) the free associative thread that begins with being cold, continues with him entering a bar to warm up with a drink, and then all of sudden he admonishes us about excess, about how excess can lead you down the drain, from where no one will save you, (5) the miraculous swing back toward metamorphosis, in this case from a human to a condor falling down because of its failed moral motor, (6) the concluding self consciousness about the usefulness of his advice — you wouldn't be able to imagine him analyzing this epigraph because you didn't come back, Ada — yes I would he hasn't changed that much — how would you know? — y ojalá que lo que estoy escribiendo le sirbalguno para que mire bien su comportamiento, Eva reads, y que no searrepienta cuando es tarde y ya todo se haiga ido al corno por culpa suya.

Part II

Elsi's Nephew

I thought the abductor was calling to say my time had come, Elsi says, my time has come, I would say to myself whenever my device transmitted its ridiculous ringtone, which ringtone, Antonio says, what is love / baby don't hurt me / no more, Elsi says, laughing, and here Eva rewinds her father's interview with Elsi so she can hear him laugh too, I used to dance to that song either in high school or when I first arrived to the United States after high school, Antonio says, my older brother used to listen to that song that's why I chose it isn't it strange to remember anything, Elsi says, you're a good singer, Elsi, Antonio says, the other day for instance I was on a bench outside a bookstore and a Christmas carol started playing in my head for no reason, Elsi says, which bookstore, Antonio says, the Fondo de Cultura Económica on Tamaulipas, Elsi says, what was happening when you heard the Christmas carol, Antonio says, the afternoon clouds were foreboding rain and everyone, Elsi says, I mean the ones without umbrellas, seemed to be doing a sad calculus in their heads, run dry now or run wet later, Antonio says, right and then I thought as soon as my brother comes out of the bookstore we will run to the bus stop except my brother has been dead for more than fifteen years, Elsi says, laughing, yes, Eva thinks, every time Elsi laughs her father laughs too, I can understand when we output a memory based on an input, Antonio says, but when there's no input I agree the brain mechanism is baffling, I thought you said you were a novelist not a computer programmer, Elsi says, I used to be a database analyst in San Francisco don't tell anyone, Antonio says, perhaps humans contain code that stipulates if no input available then output a random memory so as to make us feel less like blank robots, Elsi says, are you sure you're not a programmer yourself, Antonio says, laughing, what.is.love, Elsi (as a robot) says, you were saying you thought the abductor was calling to say your time had come, Antonio says, i.thought.he.was.calling.to.say.my.time.had.come, Elsi says, we.can.do.whole.interview.in.robot.voice.no.problemo, Antonio says, Jonathan Smith, Elsi says, the abductor was called Jonathan Smith and he was calling to say my nephew was in detention and do I want to claim him while he awaits his deportation proceedings, how did he obtain your number, Antonio says, my nephew had my number carved on his belt, Elsi says, but one of the numbers had blurred so Jonathan Smith, can you believe his name, all Pale Americans are called Jonathan Smith, Antonio says, to simplify the data entry at KKK headquarters, Elsi says, Jonathan Smith to the nth power, Antonio says, where n equals 46.1% of USA, Elsi says, so one of the numbers had blurred, Antonio says, so Jonathan Smith said he had to dial a few times before he found me, Elsi says, how many phone permutations, Antonio says, what is this math homework, Elsi says, obviously, Antonio says, ten permutations at most, profe, Elsi says, very good, Ms. Elsi, you can take your seat now, Antonio says, where should I take my seat to like the junkyard, Elsi says, careful you're scaring the other inanimate objects in our classroom, Antonio says, should I write Down with Junkyards on the board 500 times, Elsi says, yes and the rest of you children need to quiet down this is a classroom not a play yard, Antonio says, and here Eva tries to imagine his father pretending to be a stern teacher to his imaginary students, Jonathan Smith said we've captured your nephew, Elsi says, no, what Jonathan Smith said, I swear I remember his every word, profe, he said I am calling to inform you we're in possession of a child who claims to be your nephew, but I didn't tell him I had forgotten about my nephew, or that it had been months since my sister had called me and said she wanted to send her son Felipe across the border before he was shot or kidnapped in San Salvador can you imagine if I had changed my number due to a wireless switch your line for free special, for instance, you didn't talk to your sister again after she called you about Felipe, Antonio says, I love my sister, Elsi says, of course, Antonio says, I love my sister and I know that's what I'm supposed to say because she's my sister, Elsi says, but I say I love her because I do love her, even though she was taken away by the American abductors when I was still little and I, well, sometimes I think I can remember her, but I was three and she was seventeen so that's not possible you're lucky you were born in the United States, my sister would say whenever we spoke on the phone, but I didn't feel lucky, and she didn't feel lucky, and so we rarely spoke on the phone to avoid any talk of luck, so when she called you about Felipe why did you agree to receive him, Antonio says, that's a stupid question, Elsi says, you're right I'm sorry, Antonio says, I said to her sure two people can fit in my studio apartment tell your son to call this number when he arrives, Elsi says, and then I forgot, or perhaps I was expecting my sister to call me to tell me he was on his way, but she didn't call me and months went by and then one day Jonathan Smith dialed ten permutations at most and said a child who claims to be your nephew, a child who claims his name is Felipe Arteaga and that you are his aunt, and here Eva hears Elsi crying and tries to imagine what his father might be thinking because he doesn't say anything to console her — what could I have said to console her, Eva? that the world isn't what it is? — although he does soften his voice when he, after a minute and thirty two seconds, according to the program streaming this recording through the console above Eva's bed, asks her what she studied in college, algebraic topology, Elsi says, the mathematical study of Topo Gigio, Antonio says, sum.mation.of.topos, Elsi says, listen, I know what you want to know, Elsi says, I want to know everything, Antonio says, I know you are not interviewing me to learn about algebraic topology, Elsi says, who doesn't treasure the opportunity for free math lessons, Antonio says, I also know you're asking me unrelated questions to give the impression, once you transcribe this interview and shape it into a stirring monologue, that I exist outside of what I did to my nephew, yes, here's a rounded version of a human like you and me and so on, human to the nth power, Antonio says, Tata, Eva says, a blank robot to the nth power, Elsi says, so Jonathan Smith called me and my first thought was, because by then there were already reports about the abductors hiring data science vendors who would merge data from our devices with transactional data amassed by former NSA employees to locate their deportation targets, my first thought was the abductors know my location, Elsi says, I think by then they were already running probabilistic models borrowed from epidemiology to create all sorts of data linkages, Antonio says, I remember thinking if they know my phone number, Elsi says, the abductors can type it into their database, match it with a device ID, and query the coordinates of my device, so you switched off location services, Antonio says, yes but I knew they probably already had my location history so they could simply query the last twelve months and narrow down their target location to the coordinates with the most activity, so you gave your number to your sister before the abductors began to amass this kind of data, Antonio says, yes, Elsi says, and yes, by the time Jonathan Smith called me there were already reports that the American abductors were trying to meet their aggressive quota of deportables by capturing people when they appeared at the detention centers to claim their family members, but you were safe since you were born in the United States, Antonio says, I was but when I was in college, Elsi says, my freshman year at Columbia I couldn't make ends meet so I requested food stamps for like a month, so they stripped you of your citizenship, Antonio says, the law had already passed that if you had received government benefits you could be denied citizenship or could be stripped of your citizenship, but I hadn't received any notice yet so whenever the phone rang I would say to myself my time has come, or I would say to myself some kid out of college is probably at a data center in Utah right now loading the time series of the food stamp data, one state at a time, and once that's done some other kid out of college will join the food stamp data with the ethnicity data and create a file that includes me, and yes, by the time Jonathan to the nth power called me I had already seen all those terrifying photographs of the detention centers, the children in cages, Antonio says, the children fainting from dehydration, Elsi says, the outbreaks of vomiting, diarrhea, respiratory infections, the forceful injections to keep them quiet, how old was Felipe, Antonio says, I remember waking up at 2:00 AM one night, wondering if the American abductors had just awaken me up to hand me my allotted meal, a half frozen bologna sandwich, Antonio says, which was served, Elsi says, according to the news, at 10 AM, 5 PM, and 2 AM, how old was Felipe, Antonio says, he must have been seven or eight years old, Elsi says, okay, Antonio says, do you have children, Elsi says, two daughters, Antonio says, what are their names, Elsi says, and here Eva pauses the recording and considers fast forwarding it because she knows this part by heart — play it one more time, okay? — Ada and Eva, Antonio says, do you remember them at seven or eight years old, Elsi says, I remember when Ada was eight and Eva was five we attended a dance performance where a gaunt woman who looked like a ghost stumbled around while a sad looking man in a black suit opened a path for her by casting aside the chairs on the stage, Café Müller by Pina Bausch, Elsi says, that's it, Antonio says, and when we arrived at home that night Ada closed her eyes, extended her arms like a somnambulist, and pretended to be the gaunt ghost woman while Eva swatted Legos out of the way, Felipe, Elsi says, tell me about him, Antonio says, there's not much to tell, Elsi says, I don't know anything about him, okay, Antonio says, because I was scared they would detain me if I showed up to pick up my nephew so what I told Jonathan Smith, I hope you're recording this, Elsi says, I am, Antonio says, because what I told Jonathan Smith is I don't have a nephew, Elsi says, I don't know any Felipe, you must have dialed the wrong number.

Ada's Father

Or the video by Doctor Sueño that had removed all the original images of her father's abduction and replaced them with images of American skyscrapers as seen from above, Ada thinks, a memorial for my father maybe what do you think, Ada says, I was just making fun of your father's office job, Doctor Sueño says, although if she were commissioned to design a memorial for her father, no, her father isn't dead she isn't going to think about memorials now, Leonora, Ada says, call my sister again, don't think about a pink memorial, Doctor Sueño says, I am not thinking about a concert hall like a detention center, Ada says, vacant except for a live performance of Messiaen's Quartet for the End of Time or a recording of it streaming through a reverse bug, or not vacant but populated by subscribers to Popular Mechanics or Psychology Today — we wandered through the halls searching for bathrooms shaped like solitary confinement cells but the concert hall turned out to be just a concert hall — wow so oblique — or a replica of an American city like Chicago or Cincinnati or whatever, which the audience will experience from a tour bus, here's the skyscraper that contained thousands of Latin American senior data analysts, empty, there's the skyscraper that contained everyone who pretended no one was being abducted anywhere, empty, stopping on plots of land with the houses missing but with plaques that contain photographs of the houses missing, photographs of blueprints of the houses missing, photographs of helicopters airlifting the houses missing, focus on the faces of the abductors inside the helicopters, Doctor Sueño says, and imagine they are not grinning, or she could run a computer simulation of the five room house she used to imagine when she was twelve years old and her father still lived with her and her sister and her mother in a small two bedroom apartment in the NOPA district of San Francisco and she still had to share a bedroom with her sister, a house her mother often talked about because she said she was tired of living in an apartment building near the University of San Francisco that resembled a dorm since our neighbors were college students who infused the air vents with cannabis and organized late night parties almost every weekend — what do they even talk about at those parties, Ada's father would say — I wouldn't know but I can imagine, Ada didn't say but would say if she was sent back in time to when she was twelve and her father still lived with them, her father slamming a hardcover on the wall so the neighbors would quiet down, her father chuckling at the neighbors' pleasant wafts of weed, her mother rushing to shut the windows to no avail the smell seeping in like a cloud that was also a ghost crossing the wall inside the closet in mama's room look — not funny, Antonio — Ada imagining herself sneaking out of that two bedroom apartment and knocking on the door of the neighbor's late night party and saying hi I'm your next door neighbor I can't sleep would you mind if I join you, of course come on in, her neighbor would say, what do you talk about at these parties, Ada would say, we paraphrase Leonora Carrington sentences and pretend we came up with them, her neighbor would say, we look more like geometric figures than anything else, her neighbor's roommate would say, that's not a paraphrase that's an exact quote, Ada would say, and as Ada drives across the Bay Bridge she imagines herself again, without meaning to, sleeping in the living room of that two bedroom apartment and she's exiting her body and that version of her, blurry at first, is already at the neighbor's party, sporting the vintage silver leather jacket her father had purchased for her for Halloween, yes, she was twelve years old and had started to sleep on the sofa bed in the living room because she couldn't sleep in the same room as her sister anymore, had been sleepwalking, too, and during those first nights sleeping in the living room she would imagine or dream that her parents were being taken away from her, sometimes Mama, sometimes you, Tata, Ada says, and then I would think about Perrito dying, and then I would think about what would happen if I were left alone in this apartment, where would I run to first probably to school wait how would I climb that hill to get there I have no idea I would probably bike there, if I knew where the bike key was, I wouldn't tell the police because I wouldn't want to be an orphan, what happens if they take me, Ada's father says, Perrito talks to me he says my man is gone, my man is gone, Ada says, over and over, what happens if they take mama, Ada's father says, I cry a lot, Ada says, I hide in mama's bed, I jump out the window, and during those first nights sleeping in the living room every sound was amplified by Ada's inability to sleep or perhaps she was already asleep, hearing the footsteps in the apartment above and waiting for their owner to make up her mind — should

I have another croissant or shampoo my cat or? — hearing the chatter of the party next door like messages that no longer contain words just a rumble like the memory of freeways — I am sitting on a freeway, Alvin Lucier says, different than the one you're driving on now — good one — neither good nor bad, señor — the cars late at night that would stop across the street from the living room window so that their male occupants could pee in the bushes of the San Francisco Blood Bank, the aerodynamic flight to her five room house that had a separate wing for her so that she could be away from everyone, her new bedroom that she had sketched with ovals on the ceiling such that in the afternoon, after school, she could stretch herself on an oval spotlight of carpet and reread the Purgatory of Dreamers trilogy, her bathroom like a silo — an installation by Taryn Simon that consisted of eleven cement silos with professionals mourners inside, Ada, Eva said too many years ago, when Eva was beginning to explore her life as a conceptual artist — a five room house she often imagined as the augmented version of a house in the Sunset district of San Francisco they visited during an open house that had three bedrooms but unfortunately one of the bedrooms was more of an office where her bed wouldn't have fit, even sideways, a house they couldn't have afforded unless her father relinquished his studio apartment, also known as The Other Home — why didn't you want to give up your studio apartment, Tata, Ada messaged her father many years later, when she was already a senior at Yale — I was worried your mother would kick me out again so I kept that apartment just in case, Ada's father wrote — yesterday night I had a weird outbreak of thoughts, Ada wrote to Ms. Fern, her sixth grade teacher, a year before the abductors captured her father, I was thinking about my dreams, Ada wrote, not the ones I have while sleeping but the ones you want to come true I know my dreams won't become a reality and that is part of the reason I want my family dead and me left all alone with the pain who knew dreams could be so terrible, and of course Ms. Fern shared her letter with the vice principal, who shared it with her parents, who pretended they hadn't read it how was school today, Ada's father said, I wrote an awful letter to my teacher, Ada said, what was the letter about, Ada's father said, you won't like it's about you and Mama, Ada said, you know as a so-called novelist I dwell on unpleasant emotions on a daily basis so almost nothing will surprise me for instance the desire to escape from our parents and at the same time to be with our parents is quite common in life and novels, Ada's father said, okay Tata, Ada said, relieved it was okay to want her parents dead, and many years later, when she was already a senior at Yale, she asked her father about that letter and he said that her mother had been disconsolate after reading it, because she had done everything for you and your sister, Ada's father said, she even moved your bed to the living room so you could sleep better even though I was opposed to it, how about you, Ada said, I told your mother perhaps your disproportional reaction to whatever you were feeling as a eighteen year old trapped in a twelve year old's body, as you wrote in your letter, was a result of what you went through when you were three years old, Ada's father said, the strain of those months when your mother and I were separating, because during those months I became paranoid that your mother was trying to take you away from me so at night I would drive us to the pool at the JCC so we could spend more time together, just the two of us, and I remember the pool was often empty except for a Russian grandmother who would praise me for being there for you, even though I was the one who had tried to flee from you, that doesn't sound so bad, Ada said, at home your mother was often prostrated on the sofa bed, Ada's father said, unable to move, and as Ada drives across the Bay Bridge she wonders why her parents or Ms. Fern or the vice principal didn't link her letter to the anti-immigrant tirades of the Racist in Chief, who had been elected that year and had demonized Latin Americans during his presidential campaign and had mobilized his government agencies to persecute Latin Americans like her father — is he going to try to kill Tata, Eva said the morning after the first Racist in Chief won the elections — and for years she didn't link her letter to the first Racist in Chief either, imagining, instead, that the letter had been a premonition, that she, a seasoned time traveler, had gone back in time to prepare herself for her father's capture — I really want someone to hurt me so I can be stronger, Ada wrote in her letter to Ms. Fern, I can't seem to do it by myself I tried by cutting my wrists but I'm a coward — but I haven't tried to cut my wrists, Ada said — you need to stop reading those dream books, Ms. Fern said — dream books that contained mining (the pulling of dreams), seeding (the planting of dreams), sleeping shells like coffins, different selves on different bodies, no parents anywhere, of course, because they were all dead, and yes, when a year later the American abductors captured her father she did feel responsible, as if she had willed his capture by writing that letter, and after the rallies and the protests to save her father yielded nothing but maudlin reassurances and her father was deported to Colombia she didn't cut her wrists or draw an X with a knife on her heart, as she'd written in the letter, but one night, weeks or months after her father was taken away, she, asleep in her narrow bed in the living room, did try to swallow her tongue, her teeth did slice the underbelly of her tongue, she did awake in the dark with blood in her mouth and a sharp pain as if someone had shot a pellet of salt on her tongue — I rinsed my mouth and the red on the sink reminded me of trounced boxers, Tata — trounced, eh? — I knew you would like that word — and the next morning, as her mother reenacted her daily breakfast routine as if nothing was the matter inside the two bedroom apartment where Ada and Eva remained until they graduated from high school, she searched online for biting your tongue while sleeping cause of and found an article about nocturnal seizures, and because she associated seizures with both epilepsy and a scene in the Purgatory of Dreamers in which a girl has a seizure inside her sleep shell and the doctors administer an antidote through an IV, she wondered if unbeknownst to her she was living a double life, one as a middle school student who pretended nothing was wrong during the day and one as an epileptic at night — the United States is a nation of epileptics, Ada — Ada asleep and not asleep on her narrow bed in the living room, Doctor Sueño says, from where she can see the past present future — I don't sleep in the living room anymore don't be melodramatic, Ada says, or rather I do but not in that narrow bed, Leonora activate random Carrington generator, Ada says, her dressing gown was made of live bats sewn together by their wings, Leonora Carrington says, the way they fluttered one would have thought they didn't much like it, or plaques on all immigration detention centers across the United States that read future Topography of Terror museum, Ada says, and even after my dentist molded a mouth guard for me I still would sometimes wake up with blood in my mouth, Ada thinks, Leonora random generate again, please, Ada says, for forty years I've hidden behind this pile of oranges in the hope that somebody might pinch some fruit, Leonora Carrington says, again, Ada says, again.

Interpretations

In today's episode of Our Imaginary Lives Without Doctor Sueño we will be interpreting Elsi Arteaga's dream of a robot & a teacup, Doctor Sueño says, how do we know this episode isn't a dream, someone says, why does it matter if it is or it isn't, someone else says, I'm afraid of winged humans I don't want to see any of you grow wings all of a sudden, someone says, we promise not to fly away if we grow them we'll just fan you with our flutter, someone else says, I don't believe in group dream interpretation, Doctor Sueño says, and I don't believe in individual dream interpretation therefore today's episode is cancelled, jokes do pass the time Doctor Sueño said ha ha, someone says, I won't be able to remember your names, Doctor Sueño says, so I will assign you names at random you will be Auxilio Lacouture, you will be Amparo Dávila, you will be Leonora Carrington, can I be Remedios Varo instead, Leonora Carrington says, last night I dreamed I wasn't a leopard can we interpret that while we set up, Auxilio Lacouture says, to dream of leopards trying to escape from you denotes that you will be embarrassed in business or love, Remedios Varo says, does trying to escape from a leopard count as not being a leopard I think it does, Amparo Dávila says, what is the opposite of leopards trying to escape from you, Auxilio Lacouture says, a robot is about to drink tea for the first time, Doctor Sueño reads, the whole country is watching since this is a show about robots doing things for the first time, but the robot pauses, teacup in hand, for too long, so we, the audience, become alarmed, oh no the robot doesn't know what to do next, but somehow we realize the robot has paused because the robot's remembering its beloved, who happens to be a body part, the dream isn't very realistic because robots, if programmed properly, Amparo Dávila says, always know what to do next, Amparo is speaking out of turn send her to the principal's office, doctor ZZZ, Auxilio Lacouture says, Elsi's the robot's programmer, Remedios Varo says, so Elsi must have deleted the lines of code pertaining to what to do after holding a teacup, Elsi obviously programmed her robot to avoid embarrassment, Auxilio Lacouture says, because the tea would have dripped all over her metal self since robots don't have mouths, my grandmother used to interpret dreams by focusing on the most dreamlike element of the dream, Remedios Varo says, the most dreamlike element here being that there's a robot, Auxilio Lacouture says, or rather the most dreamlike element in the dream is that the audience somehow realizes the robot is remembering its beloved even though there's no outward signs that the robot is remembering its beloved, Remedios Varo says, perhaps the price of admission to the robot show included an implant of robot cues, Amparo Dávila says, so while the actions in the show seem to lack cause and effect they don't lack drama since the implant activates dramatic cues at the critical junctures except the cues don't explain themselves they just relay statements like the robot has paused because of thinking about its beloved, the opposite would be leopards charging toward you, Auxilio Lacouture says, plenty of robots are built with mouths though, Remedios Varo says, Elsi Arteaga is that you on the line, Doctor Sueño says, I thought you said you were going to ask me easy questions, Elsi Arteaga says, what happened during the week you had the dream about the robot & the teacup, Doctor Sueño says, I don't want to slant your interpretations with my own contextual infamies, Elsi Arteaga says, would you characterize your robot dream as a nightmare, Doctor Sueño says, I was terrified when I awoke, yes, Elsi Arteaga says, what comes to mind when you remember the teacup dream now, Doctor Sueño says, the robot is sitting in a room that reminds me of the room in that old sitcom by David Lynch, Elsi Arteaga says, Rabbits, Auxilio Lacouture says, to dream of rabbits frolicking about denotes that children will contribute to your joys, Remedios Varo says, see also entry for Hares, does your dream also have a laugh track that goes off seemingly at random, Amparo Dávila says, now that you mention it I think so, yes, Elsi Arteaga says, so to decode the dream we need to decode the logic of the laugh track, Remedios Varo says, did Amparo just plant the laugh track in Elsi's dream I think she did, Auxilio Lacouture says, we are projecting Rabbits on the wall here so we can log the appearance of the laugh track, Doctor Sueño says, laughter after Jane the Rabbit says what time is it, Amparo Dávila says, laughter after Jane the Rabbit says there's something I would like to say to you, Suzy, Auxilio Lacouture says, if you see a hare escaping from you in a dream you will lose something valuable in a mysterious way, Remedios Varo says, I have always imagined you transmitting your show from a bunker in Eastern Island, Elsi Arteaga says, we can't reveal our location all our signals have been scrambled to avoid detection by the American abductors, but I've already been abducted, Elsi Arteaga says, so has everyone else in this bunker, Doctor Sueño says, a bunker that also looks like the room in that Rabbits show, Remedios Varo says, we don't rely on ominous music for effect though, Auxilio Lacouture says, we have us another caller you're on the air, Doctor Sueño says, I have never understood the expression you're on the air, Amparo Dávila says, I don't understand the expression I have never understood because it implies perfect recall of what you have previously understood, Auxilio Lacouture says, to dream of air denotes a state of withering and bodes no good to the dreamer, Remedios Varo says, someone take away Remedios's dictionary of dreams, Amparo Dávila says, to dream that you are referring to a dictionary signifies you will depend too much upon the opinion and suggestions of others for the clean management of your own affairs, Remedios Varo says, I'm on speakerphone with my fellow members we're calling from Eastern Island are we neighbors, Lilian Serpas says, should I say it or are you going to, Doctor Sueño says, jokes do pass the time Doctor Sueño said, Auxilio Lacouture says, her fellow members of the imaginary island neighborhood of Tlön, Amparo Dávila says, members of The Observers of the Interdependence of Domestic Objects and their Influence on Daily Life, Lilian Serpas says, I have a secret, Jack the Rabbit says, the teacup in the dream is at epicenter of interpretation, Lilian Serpas says, because the robot has been programmed with the rules of interdependence and so the robot knows that emptying the teacup equates to refilling the iron, which does not need refilling, a coincidence, Jack the Rabbit says, just like there is no band perhaps there is no audience just a recording of an audience, Amparo Dávila says, I've received a cue from my implant that the time has come for our guests here in our bunker to lucid dream their way into new interpretations of Elsi Arteaga's dream, Doctor Sueño says, laughter when Jane the Rabbit says oh, Auxilio Lacouture says.

Elsi's Nephew

I said I am calling about Felipe Arteaga, Elsi says, you called Jonathan Smith, Antonio says, but I didn't call him from my device, no, Elsi says, at first I thought of locating a pay phone far enough from where I lived, where did you live, Antonio says, are you recording this on your device they can monitor our devices do you think their voice recognition software can detect me, Elsi says, why are you concerned about being detected here in Mexico City, Antonio says, it's irrational I know, Elsi says, but sometimes I imagine them tracking me here to notify me I am not far enough away from them, so you tried to locate a pay phone, Antonio says, I tried but you know even then there weren't that many pay phones left, Elsi says, and the ones that remained were already probably monitored by the American abductors I know I sound paranoid, hard not to be paranoid when the primary immigration objective of the United States was to expel us, Antonio says, us Latin Americans, yes, Elsi says, I remember when I would start to type my useless anti-abduction essays, Antonio says, what were those essays like please don't abduct us we already paid for our yoga classes in advance, Elsi says, my mother was a yoga instructor, Antonio says, and when I was little she would take me to her yoga classes in the forest, please don't abduct us we already paid for our yoga tours in the forest, Elsi says, pretty much, Antonio says, so you would start to type your pro yoga essays, Elsi says, oh so now you're the interviewer, Antonio says, please speak the names of your pets clearly into the mic, Elsi says, Perrito, Antonio says, Burrito is not an acceptable pet name, sir, Elsi says, so I would type one sentence, Antonio says, that is definitely not an acceptable pet name, Elsi says, time for your walk I Would Type One Sentence, Antonio says, no typing on the carpet, I Would Type One Sentence, Elsi says, so I would type one sentence, Antonio says, and I would worry that the American abductors, through my device, were going to scold me, extirpate what you typed put your hands behind your back, Elsi says, and sometimes I would imagine having fervent conversations with the American abductors through my device, Antonio says, don't you like my prose style do you want some hibiscus tea please don't report me, Elsi says, one night I typed the most virulent anti-Racist in Chief essay I could manage, Antonio says, quickly though, so as to avoid the distractions of paranoia, reasonable paranoia, Elsi says, and then I showered, Antonio says, put on my one suit, as if preparing for an interview, and waited for them in the kitchen, A Date with the American Abductors by Antonio José Rodriguez, Elsi says, sitting upright with my hands folded on the kitchen table like that guy in The Five Obstructions, Antonio says, you need to get out more, Elsi says, laughing, Jonathan Smith, Eva says, trying to imagine the night his father typed his anti-abduction essay and prepared for his date with the American abductors, what was the Christmas carol by the way, Antonio says, the what was the what, Elsi says, the Christmas carol that was playing in your head for no reason, Antonio says, pero mira como beben / los peces en el río, Elsi says, beben y beben / y vuelven a beber, Antonio says, my brother used to sing it to me when I was a baby, Elsi says, you have quite a memory I don't remember anything before I was ten, Antonio says, I don't remember either but my parents used to share videos of my brother singing to me, Elsi says, I'm in one of those bouncers with stars and sea lions hanging above me, I can't walk yet, and he's, wait, let me show you the one video I was able to save, and here Eva raises the volume of the recording so she can hear Elsi's brother singing beben y beben y beben y, stopping after the third beben y, as if to generate anticipation in little Elsi, who's cooing at her brother, que niña tan bella, someone says, she looks like me, someone else says, don't stop singing she's going to cry again, someone else says, what was your brother's name, Antonio says, Felipe, Elsi says, what happened to him if you don't mind me, Antonio says, I do mind I don't want to, Elsi says, no problem thank you for sharing that video you were such a cute baby, Antonio says, my brother was the first in our family to be deported he drowned trying to come back, The End, Elsi says, I'm sorry, Antonio says, I never met him, Elsi says, but I watched these videos of him so often that when I think of him I don't think oh I never met him, although I know that's what I have to tell other people if they ask, because if I say to a group of well wishers, for instance, that my brother and I used to hold hands and stroll together to the ice cream parlor and we had this skit in which I would always ask for the coffee flavor and he would always reprimand me and say you can't have the coffee flavor you're too little and I would say no your brain is too little coffee and growth aren't inversely correlated, and later the group of well wishers found out I had invented these memories, they would pity me and turn into a group of not well wishers, poor Ms. Elsi has lost her mind, one of them would say, someone call the lost & found ha ha that's not funny folks, come, Antonio, don't look so gloomy, this is the part where you say so you called Jonathan Smith, so you called Jonathan Smith, Antonio says, yes I did thank you for asking, Elsi says, I said I am calling about Felipe Arteaga, Elsi says, how did you get this number, Jonathan Smith said, I can't reveal my sources, I said, are you a relative, Jonathan Smith said, I am his mother, I said, I called his aunt two weeks ago but she claimed she wasn't his aunt, Jonathan Smith said, maybe she was scared to talk to you, I said, she should be scared, Jonathan Smith said, do they pay you extra to say things like she should be scared, I said, we thought he had no relatives left, Jonathan Smith said, we didn't know who to call I'm sorry, do they pay you extra to sound remorseful, I said, I don't know how to tell you this, Jonathan Smith said, tell it with verve, you son of a bitch, I said, no need to curse, lady, Jonathan Smith said, go lady your mother, I said, I am sorry, Jonathan Smith said, your son died last Monday.

Debugging

A Random Carrington Generator as a gift for his daughters, Antonio thinks, which he can code in his sleep since the task consists of numbering each sentence from the complete stories of Leonora Carrington and letting a random number generator choose from the numbered sentences (in his sleep Leonora might turn into his father and execute him so perhaps the expression [can do X] in his sleep doesn't apply to him? — [can't (you) do X] while dead in your sleep, though? — good one let me check with my manager —), and since periods are the sentence splitters even in Carrington, he will need to add code to avoid splitting sentences after Mr., Ms., Dr. (and here Antonio searches for Dr. in the complete stories of Leonora Carrington and finds a Dr. twenty times, nineteen out of the twenty, incidentally, appearing in a story about what to do after Russia gracefully donates a team of rats trained in operating on people, rats that, after much deliberation, are officially donated to the Psychoanalytical Association — transference from patient to rat will present unprecedented difficulties, Dr. Zodiac Pérez said, an ugly man who thought a lot about transference, Leonora

Carrington wrote —), but the Random Carrington Generator will be one setting out of many, Antonio thinks as he saves the Python code for his gift to his daughters and dials into his first meeting of the day at Prudential Investments, the most basic setting to be activated when his daughters want to escape too much sense, for instance, as Antonio has tried to do this week upon reading too many news reports about how the Racist in Chief has ordered his enforcers to abduct Latin American children from their Latin American parents as a lesson, a deterrent, don't come here even if your life is at risk or you will never see your children again, so if Random Carrington Generator equals the basic setting, Antonio types, then Semantic Carrington Generator will equal the advanced setting, which he can't code in his sleep since the task consists of establishing semantic linkage rules between any sentence (input) and a Carrington sentence (output), semantic linkage rules that can't be coded like a chatbot because chatbots are designed to answer a finite number of queries like how do you say catfish in Spanish (bagre), do you have the Prime of Miss Brodie in stock (no), how many Latin American fathers were driven to suicide by the United States government abducting their children (unknown), in other words a simple Carrington chatbot would require the input to be a question about the output — (input) what did the hyena eat? — (output) face of maid — whereas what Antonio's after is a set of semantic rules that will connect realism to surrealism, no, that's too grandiose, he will be content for now with creating a semblance of design — ladies and gentlemen, gather around, you sir, ask Leonora anything and she will respond to you from the beyond — where have they taken my son? — you see the semantic challenge with a sentence like that (and here the ladies and gentlemen crowd disperse — when did these circus people learn to speak in Python code? — let's go see the caged children instead —) is that sure, you could easily code these generators to return a Carrington sentence with the word son in it, which is no fun, or you could ground the code on the where statement so as to return a Carrington location at random, which is no fun either, but at the moment we can't think of a complicated semantic relationship beyond equivalence of subject / location, a simple equivalence that would erase any differences between a sentence like the hyena ate the maid's face, for instance, and the president ate the maid's face, unless, Antonio thinks on his motorcycle ride from Prudential Investments to where his daughters live, he converts both input / output into vectors and runs a cosine similarity measure to find the sentences with the highest similarity, leveraging techniques like Latent Semantic Indexing (LSI), Glove models, Word2Vec, and so on, dinner's ready, Antonio's former wife says, how was school today did you punch anyone in the face, Antonio says, no but I did cry for most of my recess, Ada says, one time in high school a kid poured his soda on my neck and I had to decide whether to let it go, Antonio says, which would have resulted in everyone pouring their sodas on my neck for the rest of my life, or fight, which would have resulted in no more sodas on neck, who won the fight, Eva says, that was at a boys school in Colombia a different world, Antonio's former wife says, I have a present for you, Antonio says, if it's a stuffed hummingbird I don't want it, Ada says, me first, Eva says, press shift enter three times, Antonio says, now read the output line, 1491, Eva says, these excellent nuns have taken care of her moral and worldly education, I don't get it, Ada says, one more time, Eva says, shift enter three times, Antonio says, 3087, Eva says, you won it with the number

XXXccc, my turn, Ada says, the code generates random sentences from the Complete Stories of Leonora Carrington, Antonio says, I don't remember these from any of her stories, Eva says, 2981, Ada says, as they unraveled themselves from the tendrils of some poison ivy, the story continued: my father was a man so utterly and exactly like everybody else that he was forced to wear a large badge on his coat in case he was mistaken for anybody, that doesn't make any sense, Eva says, bedtime, Antonio's former wife says, read us the one about the versatile rats, Eva says, where did you learn that word you're using it wrong, Ada says, I am versatile at using versatile wrong, Eva says, should we charge the same rates for sessions with rats or only half, Dr. Benito Wurst said, Antonio reads, where's my stuffed hummingbird, Tata, Ada says, arcades, Antonio dreams, arcade book by ZZZccc German, Antonio types on his phone at 4:13 AM, last night I dreamed that you were unveiling these arcade installations by great women from the past, Antonio types on his messaging application, wow, his friend Brenda Lozano types back, send me a more elaborate reply so I can include it in one of my fictions, Antonio types, include this lollipop emoji, Brenda Lozano types, I'm going to write No mames, Brenda Lozano said, Antonio types, great women from the past, Brenda Lozano types, perhaps be a bit more specific here like when you see a clear image in a dream so that it doesn't feel like an abstraction, I'm going to write Brenda Lozano replied with editorial suggestions for his dream, Antonio types, I'm your oneiric autocorrect ha ha, Brenda Lozano types, but the arcades in his dream were more like the marquee outside Davis Symphony Hall, Antonio thinks as he enters the Prudential Investments building, which is still empty at 7:15 AM, and whether or not his daughters were impressed by his Carrington gift (they were not), he's sure one day they will be impressed by it (even if by then the code will be obsolete), especially if his code can exist inside future voice interaction applications for cars, watches, headphones (and here Antonio types himself a reminder to add code to notify him whenever his daughters activate the Carrington generators), and because he likes to believe one day Ada and Eva will be impressed by his algorithmic gift he begins to code the Semantic Carrington Generator that morning and every morning for the rest of the week, testing it with the first sentence that comes to mind — the guard said I am going to take your son to get bathed, Antonio inputs, and I never saw my son again — but the responses generated by the LSI model aren't that relevant so he searches online for tuning + LSI, and later that week, as more news surfaces of how the United States government has been forcibly injecting antipsychotic drugs to the Latin American children they abducted — you don't need to administer these kinds of drugs unless the patient is plucking out her eyeballs, forensic psychiatrist Mark Mills said — he concludes that his LSI model isn't functioning properly due to the small training dataset (the complete stories of Leonora Carrington amount to approximately 4,000 sentences and LSI models generally require at least 100,000 sentences), and so to resolve this issue he ingests Project Gutenberg as his new training dataset, which contains 57,560 books, although his Python library only comes with 18 of the 57,560 books, the guard said I am going to take your son to get bathed, Antonio inputs (LSI method), and I never saw my son again, you've killed the moon, Leonora Carrington outputs, but she doesn't rot like your son, no, not quite right, Antonio thinks, the output relies too much on the word son for matching, the guard said I am going to get him bathed, Antonio inputs (LSI method), and I never saw him again, Juan said to himself I had better invent something, Leonora Carrington outputs, because if I tell him about the voice he might hurt it, the guard said I am going to get him bathed, Antonio inputs (Glove method), and I never saw him again, my head feels so heavy I can't think properly, Leonora Carrington outputs, and all I want is to leave immediately, you won't be seeing your child again, Antonio inputs (LSI method), Tartar is for children, Leonora Carrington outputs, you won't be seeing your child again, Antonio inputs (Glove method), I stayed where I was, hoping she wouldn't see me, Leonora Carrington outputs, but I had an uncomfortable feeling that she could see me very well with her great eye, you won't be seeing your child again, Leonora Carrington types, Antonio dreams, you've killed the voice, Leonora Carrington says, but he doesn't rot like your son, the voice is a bird that lives inside his stomach, Antonio says, what does transference mean, Tata, Eva says, it's when you wire dreams from your personal account to someone else's account, Ada says, what does countertransference mean, fa-fa-father, the voice says, XXXccc is not allowed on the bed, Antonio's former wife says, we haven't found her eyeballs yet, forensic psychiatrist Robert Rwatha says, stuffed hummingbirds are always in season, a stuffed hummingbird says, these excellent nuns will awake you when your time comes, Leonora Carrington says, are you my father, Antonio says, take two after every meal in a tea made of little drops of mustard in noodle water, Leonora Carrington says.

Eva's Father

I still believe you might come back, Ada, Eva thinks in the waiting room of the Hospital Luis Vernaza, still imagine you crossing the living room of our apartment on Balsamos Street but not like a ghost, no, you are you and you are crossing the living room to search for a recondite encyclopedia in the architecture section of the bookshelves above the kitchen counter and Tata is saying careful I installed that ladder myself so it might have unconscious motives, which is what he always says to me whenever I climb our sliding ladder because he doesn't know that one day, when he wasn't home, I asked the family carpenter to verify that the sliding ladder was correctly installed (it mostly was), this place reminds me of the Central Registry in All The Names by José Saramago, Tata says, haven't read it, Eva says, although she has read it but wants to see her father frown melodramatically, maybe we should attach a belt to the ladder like Senhor José does in All The Names, Eva says, tell us again about metaphorical spaces, Ada, Tata says, the immense verticality of the room and so on, Ada says, I wish I could imagine your thoughts better, Ada, Eva thinks, and perhaps I have imagined you here with us so many times not due to grief but due to I've inherited Tata's pragmatism about humans and their so-called relationships, a pragmatism that consists of acknowledging that friendships don't exist, that friends are like dummies in car crash tests except in this case they are dummies to pass the time at specific junctures of our lives, when we are in elementary school and high school, for instance, Eva's father said, and our personalities are still mostly a collection of charades, friends are a way for us to fine tune the right charades for the right occasion, and when we are in college and have accumulated what we like to call interests, we seek people with similar interests and assign them the designation of friends so we can believe ourselves when we say our interests matter, and when we are in our twenties and move to a new city we enlist whoever as sidekicks because it is not socially acceptable to meet potential lovers at bars or music festivals or parties by yourself, and when at last enough time has passed such that misfortunes are now ready to attach themselves to you, if they haven't already, most of these so-called friends recede from the landscape of your life because who has time to attend someone else's grief or insanity or infatuation with a goat, no one, no, although some pretend to do so until the pretending takes too much of their time, see for instance The Goat or Who is Sylvia by Edward Albee, the goat was the guy's girlfriend that's different, Tata, Eva said, the goat represents the limit of what's acceptable to pretend to care about for instance when I started publishing my research on the American abductors, Eva's father said, acquaintances that selected their most friendly charades for whenever they encountered me in public ceased to do so, even though they were self proclaimed progressives, except of course most of them, for the majority of their lives, had never interacted with a Latin American for more than a few minutes and so to them I was an accumulation of stereotypes, they send us their worse people and so on — we the committee for a Better South America have determined your person rating is too low to stay here please ship yourself to the United States — see? — and when I was apprehended by the American abductors and your sister's video became evidence that the government of the United States was targeting critics of its abduction policies, they probably said to themselves, or posted what they said to themselves anonymously, that Latino probably deserved it, you know what those Latinos are like, we wasted so many charades on him, and so in my experience, when it comes to humans and their so-called relationships, the only relationships that remain after the end of charades are the interplanetary ones, mom, dad, sisters, Eva said, see you on Neptune, Eva's father said, and after Eva graduated from Yale and enough of her relationships with her fellow Americans had concluded as her father had predicted, she added his prediction to the list of reasons why she should leave the United States, although there was no list, no columns with pros and cons, no letters to the editor, one day she just stashed her clothes in a duffel bag, sealed eight boxes with books, etc., and on the plane to Bogotá she didn't sleep but did draft the instructions for Hypnagogia — merge your hallucination with the first creature that comes to mind, Eva's instructions had read, and carry it to the next module — please refrain from making a scene, the instructions on the walls of the Hospital Luis Vernaza should read, Eva thinks, closing her eyes and merging her talking sunflower carrying a briefcase with a sign that says we regret to inform you every day someone dies here and yes we acknowledge the unique characteristics of your dying someone nevertheless please refrain from making a scene our nerves are too frayed already p.s. what's in the briefcase, the adventures of the face eating hyena, Eva says, the one trick hyena eats faces again how wondrous and yet unfortunately not so brief, Statler and Waldorf say, where did you two come from, Eva says, I've never been fond of puppets I just don't find them believable, Statler says, I don't believe you, Waldorf says, in the next episode of the face eating hyena the face eating hyena can't tell broccoli from brains so she eats both, Eva's father says, p.s. call your sister already, right, Taryn Simon, Eva says to Taryn Simon, which is what she's named her watch, dial my sister, can't process that request who is your sister, Taryn Simon says, oh sorry call the Architect Architects and attach the sister designation to it, should I call her dramatically, melodramatically, or obliquely, Taryn Simon says, just dial her how do I switch off the humor settings, Eva says, why can't you accept me as I am ha ha, Taryn Simon says, in which I waste my breath to state the obvious, Ada's voice message says, dad had a heart attack he's not going to, Eva says, I don't know how long he'll, call me please, should I read you a line from the Carrington hyena story, Taryn Simon says, where is the doctor why did he when is he coming back, Eva says, want me to ask his watch, Taryn Simon says, enough with the jokes, Eva says, beep me and I'll beep you back, Taryn Simon says, installation idea a meteorite lands on my beloved watch, Eva says, want a wrist massage here I'll vibrate for you, Taryn Simon says, I don't understand, Ada said when Eva messaged her that she was at the airport on her way to Bogotá, fathers, daughters, planets, etc., Eva didn't say, no, she didn't say anything, didn't pick up the phone at the airport when Ada called her, did take a screenshot of her phone showing all the Architect Architects missed calls, didn't try to explain why she was leaving because what if Ada decided to join her this was Eva's idea, goddamn it, not that she didn't want Ada to come but at least not until she arrived to Bogotá and surprised her father first, installation idea, Eva writes, a room that contains all the photos, videos, and messages you should have sent to your sister but didn't, no, Eva thinks, how would that work audience members would have to submit all of their electronic communications to a convolutional neural network but the output of the algorithm would be too similar to the photos and videos she did send, why don't you send me more photos and videos of you and Tata, Ada wrote, because you don't deserve them, Eva wrote, Taryn Simon did I write because you don't deserve them to my sister, Eva says, please hold should I say affirmative instead of yes so I sound more like a robot, Taryn Simon says, I've never been fond of watches I just don't find them believable, Eva says, I am computing an anticipated response of ha ha shall I withhold it for comic effect, Taryn Simon says, laugh, robot, Eva says, as if afraid he was being observed by thousands of eyes hidden in the darkness, Taryn Simon says, who is he, Eva says, Senhor José at the Central Registry, Tary Simon says, Alternative Life #4, Eva says, how do I activate it, Taryn Simon says, Ada stashes her blueprints and sketches in her duffel bag, etc., Eva says, and on the plane to Bogotá Ada dreams of thousands of eyes hidden in the darkness, etc., our father was reading by the window, Eva thinks, and I was reading on the other side of the room, by what had been his bedroom when he was a child and was now my bedroom, and he said my mother used to say that I would climb on this very sofa by this very window and cry all day after my sister left for school, and that my mother had to ask my sister's preschool if they would take me in earlier than scheduled because of this crying business, and so because of grief I became highly educated, The End, that's already in one of your books, Tata, Eva says, the first one and the second one, Ada says, the boy by the window, Eva's father says, air and so on, Eva's father says, collapsing on the floor, ambulance, Ada says, his requirements, Eva says, no, Eva thinks, it makes no difference to imagine Ada had been in Bogotá with us because even without imagining her here she had been here do you understand?

Elsi's Nephew

You're supposed to say how could you, Elsi says, here, I will do it for you, how could you, Elsi (as Antonio) says, first let me say thank you so much for the opportunity to share my life experiences with you, Mr. Rodriguez, Elsi says, I have come to believe, after years of practice, that I can do anything, or rather that I can avoid doing anything if I outstretch enough excuses under my feet, or, since we're talking about charming recipes for inaction, you can, for instance, say to yourself I will call back Jonathan Smith tomorrow and collect my nephew, and then forget about what you said to yourself, but make sure you don't contradict yourself by saying to yourself I will not call Jonathan Smith and I will not collect my nephew because I don't want my fingerprints, which as you know were required to collect unaccompanied children in detention, to alert the kids out of college in the data centers in Utah that I am alive inside their databases, no, say to yourself I will call Jonathan Smith and I will collect my nephew, say it out loud, declaim it even, and, most importantly, let your resolve elate you, this is the turning point, you must say to yourself, this is the moment of truth,

I accept my calling, I am not afraid of being detained, caged, deported, etc., you can even download an applause track and time it so you hear the applause after you say to yourself I will call Jonathan Smith tomorrow, and then, I don't know, run errands, do yoga, reread Adam Smith, whatever, in other words let your forgetfulness absolve you: I was going to call Jonathan Smith and collect my nephew but forgot: absolved, I wasn't going to call Jonathan Smith or collect my nephew: not absolved, and this went on for two weeks, Antonio says, I started having abysmal dreams about robots, Elsi says, I have never understood why Pale Americans are so against hearing about other people's dreams, Antonio says, a robot is about to drink tea for the first time, Elsi says, the whole country is watching since this is a show about robots doing things for the first time, but the robot pauses, teacup in hand, for too long, so we, the audience, become alarmed, oh no the robot doesn't know what to do next, but somehow we realize the robot has paused because he's in love, he's remembering its beloved, who happens to be a body part, what do you think the dream means, Antonio says, when I awoke I tried to calm myself by saying it was just a TV show, everyone in your dreams is you, Doctor Sueño says, Antonio says, that's my favorite show too, Elsi says, so you called Jonathan Smith from a pay phone, Antonio says, no I purchased a prepaid device, Elsi says, paid cash so the purchase couldn't be tracked don't you want to know how Felipe died, only if you, Antonio says, respiratory infection don't you want to know why my sister didn't call me to tell me he was coming or what happened after Jonathan Smith said your son died last Monday, Tata, Eva says as she hears her father cry, do you need a moment, Elsi says, a moment would be nice, Antonio says, so your daughters were fans of Café Müller, Elsi says,

I thought you said you were going to give me a moment, Antonio says, we didn't agree on the length of the moment that has, incidentally, already passed, Elsi says, the American abductors followed me while I was driving my daughters to school, Antonio says, I wasn't going to agree to this interview, Elsi says, what for, I told myself, but I searched your name online and found your daughter's video of the day the abductors captured you, Ada was in the backseat it was Eva's turn up front, Antonio says, I had seen that video years ago but I didn't know the father in that video was you, Elsi says, I can't watch that video, Antonio says, I used to dream of your daughter's sobbing, Elsi says, I would prefer if we don't, Antonio says, I couldn't see her but I could hear her sobbing, Elsi says, I've never watched that video, Antonio says, I used to dream of your daughter sobbing isn't that strange, Elsi says, do Elsis dream of robots & sobs yes they do, Antonio says, what happened to your daughters, Elsi says, they stayed with their mother in San Francisco, The End, Antonio says, okay, Elsi says, after Eva, the youngest, graduated from college she came to live with me in Bogotá, Antonio says, what about the older one, Elsi says, Ada's an architect, Antonio says, she stayed in the United States, Elsi says, her time hasn't come yet, Antonio says, I came back for you and not for you, Eva says, fast forwarding the recording, I took the bus toward Potrero Hill, Elsi says, toward the empty warehouses there, and once I arrived I switched on the prepaid device for the first time, which I was planning to toss right after, and I called Jonathan Smith, and he said what he said, and I said what I said, The End, okay, Antonio says, can I come pick up his things, I said, irrationally imagining Felipe had brought his firefighter hat, his notebooks with doodles of beetles, his cowboy boots that were too big for him but he didn't care that's what cotton is for, his stuffed walrus, his toy soldiers, which he had meticulously stenciled alongside his mother, both of them wearing matching aprons so as to avoid splotching their clothes, all his things, Antonio, cotton, Antonio says, you never crammed cotton balls into the tip of your shoes when they were too big, Elsi says, I rely mostly on double socks, Antonio says, but of course I knew Felipe came to the United States only with the clothes he had on, Elsi says, and of course I didn't know anything about the kind of things Felipe might have grown up with, his belt with your phone number on it, Antonio says, I can already tell I will be dreaming of your daughter again tonight, Elsi says, this time in the role of the gaunt ghost woman, do you still dream of robots, Antonio says, sometimes that TV show runs in parallel to my thoughts while I work, Elsi says, algebraic topologistic thoughts, Antonio says, and here Eva pauses the recording and says to the console above her bed search for algebraic topology, homotopy, the console says, sequence of abelian groups, Felipe, Elsi says, close file of Elsi Arteaga's interview, Eva says, an interview dated October 15th, from almost five years ago, which her father bequeathed her along with hundreds of other interviews with Latin American deportees he conducted throughout the world, bedtime, bunnytown, Eva (as her father) says to herself, removing her headphones, and Jonathan Smith said we already buried your son with the others, Eva (as Elsi) says to herself, we already incinerated his things.

Part III

Roberto's Father

I'm not afraid of my story can I have the recording when we're done I can prank these people hide the recording inside these walls what do you think don't answer this is my interview, Roberto Bolaño says, greetings, my fellow whatever you still call yourselves, my name is Roberto Bolaño, which Roberto Bolaño, you say, I am the replica of the replica of Roberto Bolaño, I say, not to be mistaken with the replica of Roberto Bolaño, how are these two different, you say, is this an interview or an interrogation what is the difference I'm just confusing with you my name is Roberto Bolaño, no relation to the other Roberto Bolaño how can you be sure you are not a replica of Roberto Bolaño, you say, good one, I say, this is going to be a horror story, Antonio says, didn't I tell you not to add yourself to my interview avoid these interferences or I will switch our dial to kaput, Roberto Bolaño says, the walls are howling, these people will say after we hide the recording inside these walls we need a remote control, batteries, speakers, a drill they don't allow drills here for obvious reasons did you bring a drill I know you didn't you come here, dressed like a mourner from gothlandia, thinking

I am going to answer your questions let me see your questions, one, ask Roberto Bolaño what 2666 means, why did you cross out your first question you can reply with your hands but no audio interferences are those antlers I can't understand your hand motions turn down the volume of your hands, two, ask Roberto Bolaño why his father brought him to the United States when he was eleven years old, three, don't ask Roberto Bolaño directly about the injections at the American detention center but find a way to bring up the subject, four, how did you end up here in Bogotá, no audio interferences, please, you're missing questions five through five thousand, five, does Roberto lap in the ocean, six, does Roberto still rhyme with Alberto if Roberto is dead, seven, how will we cover the holes on these walls we'll need seascapes and of course canapés while we wait for Alberto to paint the seaspaces you want to know why my father and I ventured across rivers and borders and lacunas and Pale Effervescent Americans hiding in the bushes your capacity to imagine why atrophied long ago in your minds, dear whatever you're still called, we're mannequins we're representatives of a different class of people to you close your eyes now, do try it, don't worry I won't stitch your eyelids shut don't hide behind the bushes close your eyes blow air into your imagination ask yourself what would force you to shutter your home and strap a tire around your son close your eyes, Antonio, every night Godzilla appears in my neighborhood and knocks on my door Godzilla says I've come for the baked goods and your son and Roberto Bolaño Senior says not tonight as he hands Godzilla the bribe and the baked goods and before Roberto Bolaño Senior runs out of bribes and baked goods he flees with Roberto Bolaño Junior to where the pale people in the bushes are murmuring why come here / don't stay here, keep your eyes closed, Antonio, dear whatever you are still called you are unable to imagine a scenario in which you flee from your condominiums your ski cabins your bread and breakfasts your master premise stipulates that your preapproved comforts will protect you from Godzilla & Company unless you don't meet the preapproval requirements I know you don't want to hear any of this you want the earnest replica of Roberto Bolaño you won't transcribe the rest ready, set, pause for effect, go, I am afraid, Roberto Bolaño says, please help me, what are you afraid of, Roberto Bolaño says, of people asking me what am I afraid of, Roberto Bolaño says, I don't remember his face, Roberto Bolaño says, what face, Roberto Bolaño says, the face of the guard who tried to wrench me from my father I don't remember the faces of the replicas of the guard who came to assist the faceless guard my father wouldn't let the faceless guard take me from him, do you remember what your father said, Roberto Bolaño says, under no circumstances does my son leave my side, Roberto Bolaño Senior said, you swine you come to this country uninvited you think you can dictate the terms of your entry, the faceless guard said, under no circumstances does my son leave my side, Roberto Bolaño Senior said while he shielded me with his arms I can see a replica of myself standing in front of myself and my father whose arms were locked below my neck like those metal bars that protect you from flying off the roller coaster and the replica of myself says please don't worry too much Dad this moment will be over soon, and a replica of a replica of myself appears and says to the three of us I have come from the future to tell you you are incorrect, what else does he say, Roberto Bolaño says, I had never seen a fistfight with my father in it, Roberto Bolaño Junior says, how many faceless replicas of the faceless guard does it take to restrain a father, Roberto Bolaño says, I don't recall the exact number they replicated themselves and kicked my father until his sprawled body on the floor halted its movements, do you remember the sound of his shoes against the cement as they dragged him away, Roberto Bolaño says, what a ridiculous question of course I remember like claws on cement leave him alone the sedated caged people didn't howl the faceless replicas transported me to a different location that same day, what was your father like, Roberto Bolaño says, my father was an astrophysicist what you really want to extract from me is tender memories of my father and I so your readers can relate to this double replicate of Roberto Bolaño dear whatever you're still called if you're reading these words you won't be able to relate to me tell me a bedtime story, Roberto Bolaño Junior would say to Roberto Bolaño Senior, what kind of protagonist this time, Roberto Bolaño Senior would say, a boy, Roberto Bolaño Junior said, twelve years old, once upon a time there was a boy who didn't know if he was here or there, the father said, so the boy searched online for am I here or there and the results were really strange, what were they, the son said, we might be inside the ear of a spider, the father said, which didn't make any sense because do spiders even have ears, and if they do happen to have ears wouldn't they have hairs inside their ears, so the boy searched online for do spiders have hairs inside their ears and the results were really strange, what were they, the boy said, the absence of hairs inside the ear of the spider means you're probably inside a spider planet inside a spider galaxy, the father said, which didn't make any sense because the boy didn't remember boarding any interplanetary spider ships so how did he even get there, so the boy searched online again and the strange search results bewildered him again and again until the boy fell asleep, what are you writing down, Antonio, let me see, what is this ridiculous handwriting of yours talk about spiders, the last time I saw my father I was eighteen years old, Antonio has written down, what do I care about your father this is my interview, Antonio, my father, my strange search results, once upon a time Antonio searched online for forceful injections to tranquilize Latin American children at the American detention centers near the border and the results were really strange, what were they, Antonio Junior said, Geodon, Olanzapine, Benztropine, Clonazepam, Divalproex, Duloxetine, Guanfacine, which didn't make any sense because these were antipsychotic drugs, these were for Parkinson's, for seizures, so Antonio searched online for the side effects of these injections and the results were really strange, what were they, Antonio Junior said, the male nurse didn't look like a boxer, Antonio, the male nurse didn't look like Santa, where is my father, Roberto Bolaño Junior said, where have they taken my father, Roberto Bolaño Junior said, when will I see my father again, Roberto Bolaño Junior said, these injections are vitamins, the male nurse said, why are you hypnotizing me, Roberto Bolaño Junior said, why is the sky shrinking, Roberto Bolaño Junior said, wash under your armpits you dirty rat, the male nurse said, more, you say, you want more suffering and squalor, say it, Antonio, I'm waiting, good, you have learned to train your silence, please sit back and relax yes I know you're already sitting, Antonio, ready, set, pause for affect, once upon a time Roberto Bolaño was released from the internment camps for refugee children from Central America and while the vitamins still coursed through his brain Roberto Bolaño searched online for his father's name and the results were really strange, what were they, Roberto Bolaño Junior said, a Honduran man in the custody of U.S. Immigration and Customs Enforcement died Tuesday of injuries sustained in a suicide attempt last week, authorities said, Roberto Bolaño Gonzalez was discovered on September 19th hanging in his cell at the Adelanto Detention Facility in Adelanto, California, about 800 miles northeast of Los Angeles, authorities said, we have personnel who monitor all the facilities 24 / 7, authorities said, unfortunately this individual was housed in a cell for one person, authorities said, he tied a bedsheet around his neck to hang himself, authorities said, and that, as you know, happens very quickly.

Auxilio's Daughter

I said to myself I think you're scared of the algorithms, Auxilio, Auxilio wrote, if you call this Antonio individual from your device, I think I thought, which is registered under my name, and you reach him on his device, which is probably registered under his name, you will awaken the American algorithms, but why have you come to imagine the algorithms as mechanical spiders, Auxilio, I said, please give me a minute to consider your question, I said, Auxilio will call Antonio, I think I imagined, the designated algorithm will crawl out of its slot and establish a linkage between Auxilio and Antonio, verify prior linkages between Auxilio and Antonio, monitor our linkage and wonder (I know wonder isn't the right word for what these algorithms do but an agglomeration of if statements does, eventually, equate to wonder, I think, and so perhaps I could write that the designated agglomerative algorithmic spider would monitor us and wonder) why our calls only lasted seconds, because I had imagined calling you and hanging up, Antonio, calling you and not speaking, calling you and transmitting the sound of the sea, which is the sound of sleep, and I know that sounds ridiculous, Auxilio, I said, you're too old for these telephonic hoaxes, for this prolonged mania of not speaking, even though I do speak, Antonio, just not to anyone alive here in Lisbon, and I know that admitting that I rarely speak might elicit pity from others, as if speaking was a brave feat, a magnificent signifier of sanity, poor Auxilio muted by misfortune, no, I didn't go mute, Antonio, I was always inclined toward not speaking, even when I was a child, I think I remember, I wrote a note to my parents saying I will not speak for a week as penance for my sins, which was odd because we were not religious, so I've wondered if perhaps that penance was a trial run to see what it would be like to not speak, speak up, my teachers would say, speak up, the slogans would say, and if the voice detection algorithms of the American surveillance agencies would have been more advanced back then I think more Latin Americans would have gone mute, more slogans would have been retired sooner, don't speak up or you will awaken the algorithms, can you imagine, as I have imagined, our voices stored inside the enormous data centers of the American surveillance agencies in Utah, Antonio, like neutrons inside nuclear facilities whispering to each other where is this centrifugal ride taking us, my voice (in data storage) reading to Aura, my four year old daughter, when insects sleep they are wakened only by poetic forces, what are poetic forces, Mama, Aura's voice (in data storage) says, can you imagine, as I have imagined, parachuting yourself to the data centers in the deserts of Utah, as if part of an adventure tour, and asking the receptionist for all of Aura Restrepo's recordings in stock, yes, I have imagined not only obtaining the recordings but creating a channel online with her recordings plus a recording of myself saying if you have heard this voice please contact me, if this is your voice please contact me, Aura, and of course I know Aura's voice has probably changed by now, but what if it hasn't, no, I know it has, Auxilio, our Aura turns twenty four this year her voice changed long ago, while you were imagining the adventure data tours of the future (because it isn't hard to imagine that one day, if humans still exist, someone will offer tours of the data centers of the surveillance agencies of the United States, although perhaps the lizards of Utah have already started organizing these tours for themselves sign up now and crawl through millions of human voices without worrying about any of these voices shouting look, mama, a dinosaur, as Aura once did upon encountering a lizard at Marine Park in Venice, California, her voice unchanged), her voice changed, and you might be wondering, as I would wonder if I were you, what about your own repository of photos and videos of Aura, Auxilio, ay Antonio, I would have said, still inside the device I lost during my deportation eighteen years ago, still swimming with the stingrays in the Pacific Ocean, and as I considered your potential questions about Aura and my own deportation, I remembered watching your daughter's video of the American abductors apprehending you, Antonio, and I thought what happened to you wasn't that different from what happened to me: the abductors captured you as you were driving your daughters to their elementary school, the abductors captured me as I was driving to pick up my daughter at her preschool, and so I thought perhaps you wouldn't want to know the external particulars of my deportation, of how I was captured and transported and caged and the rest of the brutal operation, because that would be too familiar to you, and so I thought what I should attempt to describe for you is how my mind changed after they abducted my daughter and I was deported, and I remember I imagined being part of a collective mind, the mind of all of us who have been deported and whose family members have been abducted, a mind like a sea struck by a meteor, a sea that ceases to be blue or green as it overtakes the continents, the fish turning into lizards and the lizards into birds with gills, a sea that is no longer the sea but a carnival of destruction and a cemetery and a neighborhood where I might run into you, Antonio, and I said to myself you've just had a vision, Auxilio, don't be daft focus on how your mind changed, I said, okay, I said, I'll talk about my insomnia, I said, I didn't have insomnia before my deportation but I did after, an insomnia that persisted for so long that everything in my life became a potential enemy: if I eat this sugar cookie, I would say to myself, if I exercise too much, if I read about the war between the winged lizards and the mechanical spiders too late at night, I might not be able to sleep, which was ridiculous because I wasn't able to sleep anyway, but perhaps our minds have been codified to invent causes if no causes can be located, just as our minds have been codified to avoid memories of meteors, of tsunamis, of bands of Pale Americans persecuting Latin Americans, which is probably why I have avoided telling you about the one crucial difference between our deportations, tell him, Auxilio, I said, he wants to know, after the abductors captured you, Antonio, your daughters were able to stay with their mother, whereas after the abductors captured me my daughter was not able to stay with anyone she knew: can you imagine, as I have imagined, how Aura remembers that moment, the moment the American abductors or the accomplices of the American abductors, towering over her, asked her where she lived, who was her mother, where was her mother, did she have family she could stayed with, and Aura saying, as I had asked her to say if I didn't pick her up from school or if men wearing fake police vests tried to detain her, my name is Aura Restrepo, I am an American citizen, my mother's name is Auxilio Restrepo and my aunt's name is Maria Restrepo and her phone number is 415-672-6524, and sometimes when my device rings I still think I will hear Aura saying I forgot the number, Mom, I'm sorry I'm so late but I'll be home for dinner, because Aura must have forgotten my sister's phone number, Antonio, we practiced her saying Maria's phone number, one skinny piggy between the 4 and the 5, the 6 and the 7 were married twice, that sort of thing, and just in case I had written the number on the labels of her dresses except the numbers must have faded from the dress she was wearing, or she forgot the phone number was on the labels, I don't know, Antonio, can you imagine, as I have imagined, how Aura remembers that moment, if she can still remember that moment, the moment she forgot one number out of ten, two out of ten, because of one number I lost my mother, Aura probably says to herself, but perhaps once she arrived at the detention center the American abductors injected tranquilizers into her mind and her memories of me vanished, and perhaps the American abductors transported her to a foster home and she was adopted by well meaning Pale Americans, I don't know, Antonio, I told my abductors that my daughter was at Buen Dia Family Preschool, told them the address, asked them if I could call my sister so she could pick up Aura, and I have become convinced, even though I know it's irrational, that the American abductors and I spoke a different language, not as in Spanish vs. English but as in two different species unable to make their undertandings intersect, because I said what I said to them and they replied with nothing, as if they were bored of listening to the nonsense speech of Martians, and I could see myself becoming more agitated, shouting at them and tearing my handcuffed wrists and slamming my head against the back of their heads, don't, Auxilio, I said to myself, they will incapacitate you with horse tranquilizer and you will never find Aura, and sometimes I wonder if my insomnia is the outcome of me containing my agitation in the back of the abductors' car, as if I had a double, the Auxilio that did slam her head against them, and the other Auxilio, the one that didn't, can't sleep because she's trying to find the Auxilio that did, tell him about Aura's photographs, Auxilio, I said to myself, my sister did send me three photos of Aura before her own device was taken away when the American abductors captured her and her files were wiped out from the cloud per the executive order to delete all files created on American soil by Latin American deportees, which as you know the technology companies complied with due to it's the law, and I did post Aura's photos online and asked if anyone had seen her please contact me, and I did receive a message saying I've seen your daughter, Auxilio, and I did reply immediately and a woman named Jenny Kwan did call me, no, I said to myself, why would you want this Antonio individual to relive what happened to you it's too terrible for anyone to have to relive it, he wants to know, I said, he will forgive your handwriting and help you locate Aura, I am so sorry about your daughter, Jenny Kwan said, talking at length, as if buying herself time, I thought later, are you Latino, she said, yes, I said, that's what I thought, she said, and I heard a sound like a wave of white noise, Antonio, I heard a distant commotion, as if thousands of Americans were in the background manning an enormous intercom, we now have your coordinates, you scum, Jenny Kwan said, we're coming for you, but I have already been deported, I said, I have already been banished from your accursed country, but she wasn't there anymore, Antonio, she had already hung up.

Roberto's Father

I couldn't read his mind but I knew the doctor wanted different dreams from me, Roberto Bolaño thinks, the solemn doctor wouldn't complain wouldn't say I am tired of hearing your same dream I studied mythology astrology urology so I can interpret interplanetary dreams and the discourse of aliens and yet you come here, Robertito, week after week, with the same dream, and I tolerate it as a favor to your uncle, whom I don't even like, no, the doctor never complained about my same dream the doctor even wrote down notes every week perhaps his notes consisted of same dream / same dream / same dream / can this malfunctioning adolescent read my mind / guilt is boring, did you dream this week, Robertito, the doctor would say, yes, doctor, I would say, let's hear it, the doctor would say, faceless guards replicate themselves they kick my father until his sprawled body on the floor halts its movements, I would say, where are you in the dream, the doctor would say, I am restrained by a faceless guard, I would say, what does your father say, the doctor would say, under no circumstances does my son leave my side, I would say, what do you think the dream means, the doctor would say, when I awake I think they have taken him away again, I would say, and the knowledge that they have already taken him doesn't diminish the feeling that they have taken him again, where is Antonio, Roberto Bolaño says, it's past midnight your new friend said he will be back tomorrow, a male nurse says, he comes here, Roberto Bolaño says, dressed like a mourner from gothlandia, I don't know what that means, the male nurse says, why are you even awake shouldn't you be dreaming of antibodies trapezoids gelatin, Roberto Bolaño says, I'm trying to self induce dreams of my grandfather, the male nurse says, I want to dream of your grandfather too, Roberto Bolaño says, say to yourself I will not think of my grandfather, the male nurse says, I will not think of your grandfather, Roberto Bolaño says, now go back to your room before the robots find you, the male nurse says, I couldn't read his mind but I knew the doctor wanted different dreams from me, Roberto Bolaño writes, so I searched online for pattern of grief dreams and the results were really strange, what were they, Roberto Bolaño says, soon after the death of the loved one the patient will experience alive again dreams, followed by disorganization dreams, and, once the patient has recovered, pleasant dreams, I am having a picnic on a meteor and my father approaches me and says sorry I am so late, Roberto Bolaño Junior wrote, I am washing my school uniform by hand and my father appears and says don't use it as a hat until it has dried completely, Roberto Bolaño Junior wrote, I am drawing circles for an assignment on circles and through a speakerphone on the wall my father explains to me why we shouldn't fear the existence of black holes, Roberto Bolaño Junior wrote, sorry I am so late, Roberto Bolaño's father says, you always say sorry I am late but you're always late anyway, Roberto Bolaño says, I understand you're upset at me but it hasn't been as long as you think, Roberto Bolaño's father says, why did you come back, Roberto Bolaño says, I was hungry and I was told you would share your egg sandwich with me, Roberto Bolaño's father says, I was told to avoid certain keywords or my dreams of you would vanish from me but I don't remember which keywords to avoid, Roberto Bolaño says, I've returned to tell you it was a misunderstanding, Roberto Bolaño's father says, which part, Roberto Bolaño says, the part about being inside the ear of a spider, Roberto Bolaño's father says, I am glad you find this funny, Roberto Bolaño says, keep your voice down, the male nurse says, I am not in a condition to be finding anything but I understand what you mean, Roberto Bolaño's father says, since you're here you might as well tell me a bedtime story, Roberto Bolaño says, once upon a time there was a boy from Honduras who lived with his uncle in Bogotá and worried about his doctor ending his weekly sessions out of boredom, Roberto Bolaño's father says, so the boy searched online for grief patterns in dreams and invented thrilling grief dreams for his doctor, but the boy was so good at inventing these dreams in which his father was alive again that, when the day came for him to meet his doctor, he didn't know which dream to pick first, so the boy numbered his dreams and searched for a random number generator online, setting the minimum to 1 and the maximum to 17 (I have 17 weeks of these alive again dreams, the boy thought, which will last me until Christmas unless I'm bedridden again, so after Christmas I will have to decide whether to invent more of these alive again dreams or switch to the next phase of grief dreams known as disorganization dreams, and I will need to accumulate the right data to monitor the impact of my dreams on my solemn doctor (my dream journal will include a rating for each dream based on the doctor's engagement level so I can track any negative trends like excessive yawning, narcolepsy, ironic phrases like so your father is alive again, eh?)), did you dream this week, Robertito, the doctor said, yes, doctor, the boy said, let's hear it, the doctor said, I am drawing circles for an assignment on circles and through a speakerphone on the wall my father explains to me why we shouldn't fear the existence of black holes, the boy said, what do you think the dream means, the doctor said (I will conceal my excitement about the boy having a different dream for the first time, the doctor thought, because even the most minute reaction can revert us back to the same dream — any questions or interjections, Doctor Sueño says, even an errant word might lead us astray to far away galaxies we didn't anticipate — plus my wife says that I look like a weasel when I appear too pleased), my father is alive again, the boy said, he speaks to you through a speakerphone, the doctor said, the speakerphones are everywhere, the boy said, and this was true because after the boy had written down the dream quickly, like Robert Desnos during his sleeping fits (how many years will have to pass before I know who Roberto Desnos is, the boy thought — something to look forward to, Robert Desnos said —), the boy reread it and imagined a city with speakerphones on every wall and every flagpole so that on his way to school his father could tell him intergalactic stories or reprimand him about not his tying his shoes, don't mind the speakerphones that's just my dad, the boy would say to passerby, maybe if you learned to tie your shoes we wouldn't have to hear that annoying voice every day, a passerby would say, let's steal his shoes if he's barefoot maybe his father will shut up about his son tying his shoes, another passerby would say, very good, Robertito, the doctor said, that you're no longer stuck in the same dream means we're making progress, even though I was still stuck in the same dream, Roberto Bolaño writes.

Auxilio's Daughter

Tell him of how you started recording yourself, I said, Auxilio wrote, after I wrote you that first letter, Antonio, I dreamed of the enormous data centers in Utah, and when I awoke I thought now they know I've dreamed about them, and I laughed at myself and said Auxilio if you want them to know you're thinking about them, if you want to transport yourself to the deserts of Utah and enroll in the adventure tours of the data centers, you should record yourself on your device, link your device to the appropriate wireless signals, and wait for the data centers to vacuum your voice across the Atlantic (if you search online for fiber optics + backbone + surveillance you will find diagrams of infiltrated underwater networks like a computer representation of a giant squid, and so I've come to imagine my voice coursing through the tentacles of a giant squid, tentacles that are also translucent delivery tubes like in those cartoons about the cities of the future, except this city of the future is underwater and there is no city and no Jetsons just these translucent tubes infiltrated by the American algorithms), and once the algorithms link Auxilio's Present voice with Auxilio's Past voice, which wouldn't be tough to do since my voice hasn't changed in the last eighteen years, although it should have changed, Antonio, if my mind has changed, I said to myself, how come I still emit these same hollow sounds, even in Portuguese, a meia de leite, please, um abatanado, and as I reread the first letter I wrote to you I wondered if everyone you've interviewed compares their exile to purgatory: we will punish you by expelling you, sure, and you will land in a new country and live with an aunt who will die a year later, sure, and you won't understand the language, sure, but you will almost understand the language, every day you will amble through Lisbon and you will say to yourself, in the Spanish you learned from your mother, yo sí que entiendo estos susurros, pero no, these whispers will only sound like Spanish from afar, and so during your first few years in Lisbon you will feel submerged in purgatory, in any case if Auxilio's Present and Past voice can be linked by the American algorithms, I said to myself, then Auxilio's Present voice and Aura's Past voice can also be linked, assuming they have recordings of Aura and I from eighteen years ago, which makes you wonder, as I have wondered, if the algorithms have also been able to link Aura's Past and Present voice, dear surveillance algorithms or those in charge of upkeeping the surveillance algorithms, I said into the microphone, holding it close to my mouth like Joan Jett does in her music videos, dear Antonio, I said during session #4, which I just listened to, imagine a performance of Krapp's Last Tape in which the tapes are audio files recorded on Krapp's device that the audience can hear through headsets while seated in an area that resembles the data center of a surveillance agency, dear Antonio, I said during session #10, which I just listened to, while I was an undergraduate at UCLA I wanted to pursue a major that included neuroscience and psychology and literature, and many years later, when I was already a practicing psychotherapist in Venice, California, I encountered the works of Adam Phillips, who said that for him writing about psychology is literature, dear Antonio, I said during session #11 that same evening, which I just listened to, leopards break into the temple, Adam Phillips writes, quoting Kafka, and drink to the dregs what is in the sacrificial pitchers, again and again, until it can be predicted in advance and it becomes part of the ceremony, and so what happens to something like dreaming, Adam Phillips writes, when it becomes part of a ritual like psychoanalysis, dear Aura, I said during session #1, which I don't need to listen to, if you are still alive and the voice recognition algorithms work and they have synapsed our Past / Present linkages, you and I have already reunited in Utah, dear Antonio, I said during session #12, which I just listened to, what will happen to my memories of Aura if they become part of a ritual of confession, dear Antonio, I said during session #13, which I just listened to, I've been thinking of myself as a primary node, and every moment of my life that can be converted into data as another node linked to the primary node, and one evening I closed my eyes and extended my arms and imagined reaching the nodes that link me to Aura and I said to myself that's quite the melodrama of data, Auxilio, dear Antonio, I said during session #2, which I don't want to listen to, I was thinking of the leopards while I was driving to Aura's preschool the day the abductors detained me, dear Antonio, what happens to our memories if they become part of a ritual of grief, can you imagine, as I have imagined, how Aura remembers that moment, I said to myself, rereading that first letter I wrote you, can you imagine, as I have imagined, how I remember that moment, which doesn't begin with the American abductors or the accomplices of the American abductors towering over Aura but with Aura running to the slides in the playground in the back of Buen Dia Family Preschool, running to the library in the front room of Buen Dia, back and forth, front to back, as if it was her first day of preschool and she was trying to exhaust playtime before a bell dissolved her carefree options, and here I should clarify I am not inventing parts of this moment because during her first day of preschool she did run from slides to library and back, and I did run after her with my camera, which captured on video not only her running but me saying careful with the sandcastles, Aurorora, read us about Solla Sollew, Aurorora, and in that video, which was erased by the American abductors and their executive decrees, you could hear the voice of the director of Buen Dia, a Pale American woman who had volunteered at an orphanage in Guatemala during the 1970s and who unfortunately was ninety years old when I asked her if perhaps she should secure the front door a bit better since her preschool had a Latin American name and a lot of Latin American preschoolers, if she should remove the sign up front that said Buen Dia Family Preschool, if we should establish protocols on what to do if a parent doesn't show up and can't be reached, dear Antonio, I said during session #23, which I just listened to, this agglomeration of ifs depletes me, although sometimes at night I say to myself make yourself comfortable and roll the if tapes, Auxilio, what if I forgot to write my sister's number on the label of that one dress, for instance, or what if instead of giving my sister's number to the ninety year old director I would have given it to the young preschool teachers, or what if the director did call my sister and did reach her but because the American abductors had been bribed by the American foster homes or the American adoption agencies they abducted Aura anyway, or what if she's on her way to Lisbon as I write you this letter, Antonio.

Roberto's Father

I didn't say please don't ask me any more details about the same dream, Roberto Bolaño says, or that my same dream wasn't a dream but a reenactment except for one detail, fine I'll bite, which detail, the male nurse says, please don't bite me haven't I suffered enough already ha ha aren't the robots here voice activated, Roberto Bolaño says, yes but I have a remote control and can deactivate them so you didn't tell your doctor your dream wasn't a dream, the male nurse says, why are you still awake shouldn't you be projecting your grandfather onto your forehead I did tell the doctor the dream was a reenactment but I didn't tell him the one detail that wasn't, Roberto Bolaño says, I can't sleep and I'm still an amateur inducer of grandpas so what was the detail, the male nurse says, don't you want to know the dream first, Roberto Bolaño says, I hate hearing about other people's dreams not because I hate dreams but because the retelling always removes the hallucinatory from them, the male nurse says, unless they're retold by Robert Desnos, Roberto Bolaño says, or as virtual realities of Roberto Desnos, the male nurse says, how do I know I am not in a dream right now, Roberto Bolaño says, is there a dreamlike element to this exchange, the male nurse says, you are talking to me the nurses never talk to me I don't even know your name, Roberto Bolaño says, call me Ulises Lima, the male nurse says, see that's confusingly dreamlike I am in a dream after all grow your wings and let's get out of here, Robertito, Roberto Bolaño says, I'm sorry I shouldn't have said that one of the nurses told me your name was Roberto Bolaño I'm not Ulises Lima but you can call me Ulises Lima, Ulises Lima says, Ulises Lima, Roberto Bolaño says, good boy now eat your puree and tell me about this reenactment of yours, Ulises Lima says, faceless guards replicate themselves they kick my father until his sprawled body on the floor halts its movements, Roberto Bolaño says, where are you in the dream, Ulises Lima says, I am restrained by a faceless guard, Roberto Bolaño says, what does your father say, Ulises Lima says, under no circumstances does my son leave my side, Roberto Bolaño says, did you hear that wailing on the other side I have to check the halls I'll be back, Ulises Lima says, how's our boy doing today, Robert Desnos says, the boy exhausted his alive again dreams, Roberto Bolaño's father says, but because the doctor's engagement score did trend downward by the time the boy was done retelling all seventeen of them, the boy decided to discontinue the next batch of alive again dreams and instead write a new batch of disorganization dreams, the next phase of grief dreams according to the boy's research, Robert Desnos says, dreams in which his father either says goodbye or tells his son he has to embark on a journey, Roberto Bolaño's father says, I don't want to hear about my disorganization dreams again I already wrote them I already imagined sequels for them, Roberto Bolaño says, you're hurting your father's feelings what else is he going to do he's been practicing the retelling of your dreams for weeks, Robert Desnos says, I was still dreaming the same dream, Roberto Bolaño thinks, but by the time I wrote my third disorganization dream the same dream temporarily retreated and I retrieved parallel dreams dreams that had been there all along, Roberto Bolaño says, dreams disguised as plants, Robert Desnos says, no one wants to hear my tales from the crypt dreams, Roberto Bolaño says, deadly invitation dreams according to the boy's research, Roberto Bolaño's father says, I am at an American diner and my father knocks on the window and says join me in the parking lot, Roberto Bolaño says, what's in the parking lot, the boy says, a dumpster and my grave, Roberto Bolaño's father says, so the boy searched online for meaning of father asking son to accompany him to the grave and the results weren't strange, Roberto Bolaño says, the dream meant the boy wanted to end his life, Robert Desnos says, where is my father I thought he wanted to retell my dreams, Roberto Bolaño says, but the boy didn't want to end his life, Robert Desnos says, I didn't want to end my life I hadn't thought about ending my life I wanted to sleep and awake when my father had already returned, the boy says, the boy learned from his research that if he told the doctor about this deadly invitation dream he would be dispatched to a mental institution, Robert Desnos says, and that as you know happens very quickly, Doctor Sueño says, so what was the detail, Ulises Lima says, what was all that wailing did your grandfather reincarnate as a hyena, Roberto Bolaño says, one of the robots fell over or was pushed over again and apparently one of the other nurses changed the emergency setting to wailing, Ulises Lima says, did you ever dream that your grandfather came back and told you to join him in the grave, Roberto Bolaño says, no but I did dream my grandfather came back and warned me about wailing robots, Ulises Lima says, I don't see any puree anywhere my father used to feed me he would say do you want a plane a train a spaceship and I would say a spaceship and the spoon that was the spaceship would descend from the skies, Roberto Bolaño says, whoosh, Ulises Lima says, faceless guards replicate themselves they kick my father until his sprawled body on the floor halts its movements, Roberto Bolaño says, you already told me that part, Ulises Lima says, they carried him away and when he turned to look at me his face was my face and I was relieved they were carrying me instead of him, Roberto Bolaño says, that's the one detail that isn't a reenactment, Ulises Lima says, by now that one detail is a reenactment of the first time the same dream appeared but not a reenactment of what happened at the American detention center for Latin American children, Roberto Bolaño says, do you still have the same dream, Ulises Lima says, that was twenty years ago, Roberto Bolaño says, but yes.

Auxilio's Daughter

I have been dreaming about you for the last thirty years, Ellen said, Auxilio transcribes from session #33, and later that same night, after Aura and I had driven back from the grocery store where we'd ran into Ellen, Aura interrupted the bedtime story she had invented for me and asked me what was my role in Ellen's dreams, and perhaps compelled by her newfound logic that if I knew the particulars of Ellen's dreams I must know the particulars of all dreams, even though I hadn't answered her question about Ellen's dreams yet, she asked me what was her role in my dreams, what are dreams, I said, dreams are bubbles of mind that accompany us while we're asleep, Aura said, some dream experts say dreams carry secret meanings that we try to avoid while we're awake, I said, do I carry secret meanings, Mama, Aura said, do you want to carry secret meanings, I said, only if they're not too heavy or smell funny, Aura said, some brain scientists say dreams are just synapses misfiring, I said, what are synapses, Aura said, think of cables joining each other, I said, the cables of the dream machine, Aura said, our mind is the dream machine, yes, I said, pull my left ear and my dream machine will make a dream for you, Aura said, pull completed, doctor, I said, I am a bird inside a gelatin cake, Aura said, and the gelatin cake is served and someone says what does it have inside and a voice says fruit, that's from The Gelatin and the Vulture, I said, I still have to imagine the gelatin cake so that's still counts as a dream, Aura said, Ellen was my next door neighbor when I was growing up, I said, and the summer after I graduated from high school her son and I dated for a few months, Ellen was your second mother, Aura said, I remember we were vacationing in Darmstadt because her son was attending a seminar on Messiaen there, I said, and I'm surprised at this juncture Aura didn't ask me what or who Messiaen was, Antonio (and so perhaps next time I reach this Messiaenic juncture I will pull a chronometer and measure how many seconds it takes me to fast forward to visions of Aura at fifteen or sixteen years old punning about Messiaen / Messiah, or messaging me a feral birds video from Hitchcock whenever I message her about local concerts of Oliver Messiaen's music (and here Auxilio fast forwards the recording because she doesn't feel like hearing about alternative lives alongside Aura)), I rented a Vespa, I said, avispa is wasp in Spanish, Aura said, avispate is get smart in Spanish, I said, avispate on the Vespa, Aura said, one day I avispated Ellen's son on the Vespa to see his mother, who was teaching Gestalt in a farm on the outskirts of Frankfurt, I said, and I remember she came outside to wave us goodbye as I rode her son away on the Vespa, and I remember the silos behind his mother as she waved us goodbye, and that was the last time I saw her until we ran into her at the grocery store, and that's how I have remembered her for the last thirty years, waving us goodbye, and perhaps that's the role I play in her dreams, Aura, as a symbol of youth, carefree and full of possibilities, what does Doctor Sueño think, Aura said, Doctor Sueño is already asleep, as you should be, I said, you didn't answer my other question about the role I play in your dreams, Aura said, if I was dreaming of the protagonist in The Child Jorge, for instance, I said, you would be the set or the canvas on which his head turns into a house, if you were reading The Child Jorge, Aura said, I will be the paper on the page, enough, Auxilio thinks, pausing session #33, which she recorded yesterday, dear Doctor Sueño, Auxilio thinks, please rig my dream machine for one night so I can lucid dream my way back to my daughter, sleep, Doctor Sueño says, you forgot to tell Antonio we were at the grocery store late at night because we wanted to make cookies and we needed to buy cookie dough, Aura says, please hold while we activate the voice recognition algorithms, the lizard says, you forgot to tell Antonio that due to the wildfires my preschool was closed that week and that's why we could bake cookies so late at night, Aura says, you shouldn't have been outside even with those anti-particles masks, Jenny Kwan says, you forgot to tell them I asked you what Gestalt was, Aura says, AQI equates to 275 equates to purple emergency on the air quality maps, Doctor Sueño says, take your mother to Frankfurt and ask her about Gestalt again, Ellen says, you forgot to tell them I used to memorize the books you would read to me and I would read them back to you, Aura says, don't call me a dinosaur it hurts my feelings, the lizard says, The Child Jorge liked to eat the walls of his room, Aura says, we're out of canvases, Auxilio, Antonio says, The Child Jorge swallowed all the anti-wall eating medicine his father gave him and a house grew inside his head, Aura says, why did you tell us the location of your daughter that doesn't make any sense, the abductors say, who invited those guys, Aura says, where is everybody going, the meteor says, Jorge was happy playing with the house in his head but his father was sad because passersby would say to him what a strange child you have, Aura says, my name is Aura Restrepo, Aura says, I am an American citizen, my aunt's name is Maria Restrepo and her phone number is 415-6[ ]2-652[ ], a meia de leite, please, Auxilio's says as she tries to fall asleep, but she doesn't fall asleep, damn sugar cookies, Auxilio thinks, session #34, Auxilio says into the microphone, but Auxilio doesn't know what else to say, do you dream of paintings, Aura says, not too much, Auxilio says, then why do we come see these paintings, Aura says, to see if any of them gives me clues to the riddles, Auxilio says, what riddles are you training to be prophet, Aura says, a therapy session is like a riddle let's talk about this painting, Auxilio says, I like that guy upside down on the horse and how the labyrinth seems to continue down toward like a black hole, Aura says, I like the crazy eye of the horse as if he knows where the labyrinth leads, Auxilio says, he's looking at us, Aura says, one of the horses seems to have vanished on the way to the center, Auxilio says, I like the tall orange people who are playing a hand clapping game like the ones we used to play when I was little, Aura says, session #34, Auxilio says into the microphone, dear Antonio, if the machine tasked with reconstructing what did happen is the same machine tasked with inventing what didn't happen what is the difference besides other people's requirements that it be tangible?

Roberto's Father

I don't want to forge dreams anymore, I said, Roberto Bolaño thinks, I didn't want to write or think or daydream pleasant dreams, Roberto Bolaño says, the last phase of grief dreams in which the dead are young again, Roberto Bolaño thinks, or the dead offer advice, Robert Desnos says, explain yourself, I said, as you already know, your honor, call me Roberto Bolaño, as you already know, Roberto Bolaño, I wrote seventeen alive again dreams, which equated to seventeen weeks of sessions and according to the doctor a sense of progress, then I wrote thirteen disorganization dreams, which equated to thirteen weeks of sessions and not just progress but a glimpse of a bright end in the horizon, the doctor said, the light, my uncle said, lampposts, I said, what did you say, my uncle said, the light, I said, I knew you could do it, my uncle said, we can't live in the past forever, I said, that's what I say, my uncle said, that's why I said it, I said, what did you say, my uncle said, at last you're letting go of the unpleasant past, the doctor said, faceless guards replicate themselves they kick my father until his sprawled body on the floor halts its movements, I didn't say, I think you have come to terms with your faultlessness, the doctor said, grief is boring, I said, what did you say, my uncle said, I am letting go of what I should let go not of what must go because this isn't a mattress warehouse sale, I said, he even jokes now, the doctor said, but I do think we can live in the past forever, your honor, I said, I hereby concur with the defendant, I said, everyone in your dreams is you, Doctor Sueño says, might as well tell me a bedtime story, I said, what kind of protagonist, I said, a boy who wants to live in the past, I said, for how long, I said, for a little while longer, I said, once upon a time a boy who wanted to live in the past just a little while longer also wanted to understand black holes so the boy searched online for black holes and the results were strange and so on and on, what are black holes, father, the boy said, is this one of your I gotcha quizzes, the father said, of course it isn't why would you think that, the boy said, are you recording this are you trying to make one of those Dads Against the Web videos, the father said, I wouldn't dream of it, the boy said, yes you would, Robert Desnos says, so if I look at your search history I won't find websites on black holes, the father said, did you know time doesn't pass near a black hole, the boy said, you can't be near a black hole without being drawn into the black hole, the father said, the event horizon I know but it's a scientific fact that on the rim of the event horizon time doesn't pass, the boy said, oh so a scientist has been there, the father said, it's not that time doesn't pass it just slows down I used to say to the hummingbirds in the garden slow down and at night I would wait for them to materialize in my dreams, Roberto Bolaño says, the garden here or I'm sorry I should have asked am I to remain silent today too, Antonio says, the garden in the house in Honduras where I used to live with my father, Roberto Bolaño says, good morning our Roberto didn't sleep well last night please be gentle with him, Ulises Lima says, what am I a fluffy pillow could you please check I am not a fluffy pillow I am confusing with you I knew that if the hummingbirds didn't materialize in my dreams that same night they wouldn't materialize at all I can't see the future but I can see that tonight you will search for The Hummingbirds of Honduras, Roberto Bolaño says, did the hummingbirds of Honduras ever show up in your dreams, Antonio says, not until I realized that sitting and watching them and saying to them slow down wasn't going to materialize them I had to interact with them make a scene with them so I covered myself in leaves and staked myself in the garden like a scarecrow and streamed birds noises through tiny speakers I predict tonight you will search for Bird Noises of Honduras, Roberto Bolaño says, poo-tee-weet, Antonio says, no one dreams in your novels you're going to excise my dreams from your book on American abductions, Roberto Bolaño says, Americans used to have a baffling bias against dreams and I accepted their bias without questioning it, Antonio says, your daughters tell you their dreams, Roberto Bolaño says, my youngest daughter and I share an apartment in Bogotá and we tell each other our dreams during breakfast, yes, Antonio says, tell me a recent dream your daughter shared with you or I will unleash the hummingbirds of Honduras on you, Roberto Bolaño says, be careful he's done it before, Ulises Lima says, my daughter Eva can speak all the languages in the world, Antonio says, and when she speaks Spanish to her Spanish teacher her words come out as blah blah blah, although her Spanish teacher understands what Eva's saying, there's an Eva in your first novel a time traveler she has forward backward time lapses, Roberto Bolaño says, you're the first one to notice Eva's time lapsing, Antonio says, we've had to regulate his reading of novels otherwise fantasy and reality, Ulises Lima says, for years now inhabiting in the present what she knows she will imagine in the future, Roberto Bolaño reads, I wrote this down to impress you who doesn't like to impress the experts, Roberto Bolaño says, tell him about how you used to invent dreams for your doctor, Ulises Lima says, who invented this guy, Antonio says, he wants you to interview him too I met him last night he told me his name was Ulises Lima just to confuse with me, Roberto Bolaño says, I'll interview him if he brings me a bottle of Los Suicidas, Antonio says, I used to have the same dream so I invented different dreams except I didn't want to invent pleasant dreams, The End, Roberto Bolaño says, what would be an example of a pleasant dream, Antonio says, my father's eighteen and he's organizing a guitar jam in my bedroom he's asking everyone to improvise on a tune by The Cure, Roberto Bolaño says, which tune, Antonio says, the beginning of Pictures of You then my father's seventeen he's at a record store the salesperson mocks him because he's dressed like a businessman my father says you look like a rabbit the salesperson likes my father's response so he shares a video that Robert Smith handed to him, Roberto Bolaño says, what's in the video, Antonio says, a video taken from a moving car of a country house that has gone dark, Roberto Bolaño says, what was the same dream, Antonio says, faceless guards replicate themselves they kick my father until his sprawled body on the floor halts its movements, Roberto Bolaño says, where are you in the dream, Antonio says, I am restrained by a faceless guard, Roberto Bolaño says, what does your father say, Antonio says, please forgive me, Roberto Bolaño says, Robertito, my father says, please forgive me, but I have already forgiven you, I say, please just come home.

Part IV

Juliet's Mother

I didn't recognize that creature and that creature didn't recognize me, Juliet thinks, which isn't that strange, I know, you were seventeen months old, Antonio says, I was twelve years old the first time I searched for my name online and found videos of a seventeen month old who was supposed to be me and I thought that creature isn't me, Juliet says, which isn't that strange, I know, your mother hadn't told you you'd been separated from her at the border when you were seventeen months old, Antonio says, have you seen videos of yourself as a seventeen month old, Juliet says, not videos just photographs that my mother used to store in the basement of our apartment in Bogotá, Antonio says, which used to flood so much that our paper boats floated by the armoires down there and later, when the water had drained, our apartment would smell of rotten wood, did you ever worry that the water would destroy your photographs, Juliet says, I didn't but when years later my sister lost parts of her reason in Baltimore she also lost those photographs, Antonio says, you've seen the videos of me as a seventeen month old, Juliet says, I saw you in person, too, Antonio says, oh did they assemble a grim parade for me in San Francisco at last Juliet has been reunited with her mother and you were in the crowd, cheering for me, Juliet says, an immigrant rights group had posted online that a family needed a place to stay in San Francisco and I replied that I might be able to help, Antonio says, you met me in person, Juliet says, two days after you were reunited with your mother, yes, Antonio says, I don't remember you, Juliet says, you and your mother and two social workers came to see my studio apartment but it was too small for you and your mother and your brother and too far away from your uncle, Antonio says, what was I like did I frown at you did I say you look like a hyena, Juliet says, I didn't know who you were when I offered my apartment, Antonio says, but after I exchanged some messages with one of the social workers and they told me you and your mother were coming the next day I scrolled through their postings and realized you were the baby in the video that had been circulating in the news two days earlier, Antonio says, I did recognize my mother in that video but I wasn't moved by the spectacle, Juliet says, her crying or the creature's crying, as I am sure you were, you were in your mother's arms and I said I love your pink hat, Juliet, Antonio says, did you make me cry, Juliet says, the social workers asked me not to touch you or look at you, Antonio says, do you want to see the video of that creature wailing at the San Francisco airport again before we continue so you can prepare yourself to ask me heartfelt questions so that when you listen to the recording of this interview you can hear your heartfelt voice asking me how did it feel to be separated from your mother, Juliet thinks, because of what you had been through, Antonio says, I thought perhaps the reason I didn't recognize that creature as myself is because I had already read not only about how the United States government had separated me from my mother but about the consensus about the consequences of this separation, Juliet says, and later, when I was eighteen or nineteen years old and I was, against the widespread diagnosis, thriving at UC Riverside, I watched that video of myself as a seventeen month old again and thought of the millions of Americans who'd turned into experts in childhood trauma and had concluded that I was irreversibly scarred, irreversibly traumatized, make no mistake, so many of them wrote, this child has been irreversibly damaged by this administration, make no mistake, Antonio, I despise anyone who uses the expression make no mistake, the life manuals advise us to learn from our mistakes so the expression make no mistake is against the manuals, Antonio says, you're a joker, Juliet says, my apologies I inherited a penchant for bad jokes from my father, Antonio says, I was fine, Juliet says, I was almost done with college, and even though I was going through a difficult breakup I didn't feel irreversibly anything except one day, do you want me to describe what kind of day it was, it's not necessary unless you, Antonio says, I was attending a job fair on campus, Juliet says, you know with booths and representatives wearing their business costumes and as I was about to greet the representatives of a robotics firm, you wanted to build robots, Antonio says, I was a computer science major and I wanted to write my own algorithms, Juliet says, I wrote an NLP program many years ago for my daughters a Semantic Carrington Generator, Antonio says, I didn't know which area of artificial intelligence I wanted to focus on yet, Juliet says, but I knew I wanted to automate every aspect of my life that could be automated like answering the same interview questions, for instance, retelling the same childhood memories when you meet someone new, for instance, Antonio says, no more having to exert yourself retrieving paper boats from the basement, Juliet says, my nose is broken I don't even know what rotten wood smells like, Antonio says, I would imagine a brain implant that would automate every function that didn't require our imagination so that our brain's sole purpose would be to output imaginative conjectures, Juliet says, that would veer literature toward the unknown who knows what a supermind, Antonio says, every imaginative field would veer toward the unknown plus our supermind would allow us to avoid most human contact, Juliet says, why interact with tedious humans if you can imagine interacting with compelling humans, Antonio says, in any case as I was about to greet the representatives of a robotics firm, Juliet says, three representatives from a management consulting firm ran from their booth toward a lanky Latin American student, threw him to the floor, and handcuffed him, a fake management consulting firm, Antonio says, a fake job fair, I thought, Juliet says, so I said to myself Juliet this is a trap you need to leave right now but don't call attention to yourself by running or screaming, what did the other students, Antonio says, there weren't that many students either because it was too early in the morning or because someone had tipped them that it was a fake job fair, Juliet says, so you walked out, Antonio says, I walked out and I could already see myself driving away as fast as possible but soon after driving away traffic paralyzed everything, Juliet says, Los Angeles traffic, Antonio says, fake traffic, Juliet thinks, it didn't feel like the usual traffic, Juliet says, and although I didn't think it was fake traffic I did wonder whether it had been arranged somehow to entrap me, which isn't that strange, I know, if enough time passes, Doctor Sueño says, even the most preposterous possibilities will navigate across the sea of your mind, and that's when everything went dark and I saw myself opening the door of my car and walking away, Juliet says, you left your car in the middle of the road, Antonio says, yes because I knew it was a fake road surrounded by fake cars and fake buildings, Juliet thinks, I don't want to do this anymore, Juliet says, I'm sorry if I, Antonio says, while I still lived in Los Angeles the American reporters would reach out to me every few years to see how I was doing but ever since my mother and I were deported, Juliet says, if you change your mind I'll be here in Buenos Aires for a week, Antonio says, you should be careful with what these interviews, Juliet says, but she doesn't want to hear herself speak anymore so she stands up, thinking handshake, door handle, footsteps away from the basement office of the Latin American Art museum where Antonio has been interviewing her, trying not to call attention to herself by running — I don't feel like running do you? — not while wearing these uncomfortable sneakers — and while she's transported away from the Latin American Art Museum she doesn't think the commuters in this subway train are fake commuters (because she knows she's in Buenos Aires now and no government agency here has orchestrated fake gatherings to capture people deemed undesirable — they used to throw undesirables from airplanes but that's not the same I know —), although she does scrutinize the people on the train to verify she hasn't seen them before (not that she expects to encounter anyone she has seen before since this isn't her usual route), and no, Antonio hasn't followed her, and no, she wasn't about to tell Antonio what she didn't tell the American doctors back then, when she was twelve or thirteen, when she was eighteen or nineteen, because she knew that not recognizing herself in that video at the San

Francisco airport when that creature was reunited with her mother wasn't strange, but seeing that creature glare at her was — she glared at me as if I was just another spectator — that creature in my mother's arms stopped wailing and glared at me, Juliet says, what creature, the woman sitting next to Juliet says, I'm sorry I didn't realize, Juliet says, don't worry I've been talking to my dead husband for twenty five years, the woman says, what do you say to him, Juliet says, don't forget to take out the garbage, Enrique, the woman says, don't leave your socks in the living room, Enrique, sometimes I talk to the seventeen month old version of myself, Juliet says, what do you say to her, the woman says, don't worry we turned out okay, Juliet says, does she believe you, the woman says, no, Juliet says, this is my stop, the woman says, did you follow me here, Juliet doesn't say, no, Juliet thinks, she wasn't about to tell Antonio (and will not tell Antonio since she will not be returning to the basement office of the Latin American Art museum) what she didn't tell the American doctors back then, because she's tired of other people's empathy — I told you she was irreversibly not okay — plus the seventeen month old representation of herself only didn't recognize her that first time Juliet watched the video of her mother being reunited with that creature at the San Francisco airport, and of course she watched that video again and everything in that video (the child services accomplice delivering that creature to her mother while the flash of the cameras exacerbated the staged drama of the moment, the child services accomplice exiting the frame of the video as if embarrassed she has become attached to little Juliet even though she works for a criminal government agency in charge of abducting children from their parents) stays the same except that creature doesn't glare at her anymore, that creature wails as soon as her mother holds her, resentful of her mother who has been gone and isn't gone anymore but might be gone again, that creature who wasn't old enough to tell the men hovering with their recording equipment at the San Francisco airport to leave her and her mother alone, can't you see my mother is crying, Juliet says, my mother was holding on to a tissue in her hand as if it were an orthopedic ball, Juliet thinks as she opens the door to her apartment, you're early, Juliet's mother says, I finished debugging my implants so they let me out early, Juliet says, if the implants are ready can I use them to teach my high schoolers to stop chanting their apocalyptic songs in class, Juliet's mother says, are you talking to me or the implant, Juliet says, one day we will sit together on the sofa and our implants will talk to each other all night long, Juliet's mother says, meanwhile, in our enormous imaginations, Juliet says, I've been stir frying your favorite, Juliet's mother says, did you have another dream of RIP by robots, Juliet says, what if the wildfires catch us tomorrow we might as well eat your favorite every day, Juliet's mother says, I wasn't complaining I should have modulated my response so that it was clear I was just teasing you, Juliet says, I knew you were teasing me already so if you modulated your response I wouldn't have understood the tone of your response, Juliet's mother says, your lomo saltado without tomatoes is my lomo saltado without tomatoes, Juliet says, especially if you're constipated, Juliet's mother says, should we continue our chess match while we eat did you move any of the chess pieces do I have to check the photo of the chess board again, Juliet says, I didn't but even if I did shouldn't you let your old mother win every now and then, Juliet's mother says, yes mother, Juliet says, you don't mean that, Juliet's mother says, no mother, Juliet says, are there algorithms already that can predict your personality type based on your chess moves, Juliet's mother says, an overreliance on horses is a predictor of a digressive personality recommendation.equals.do.not.hire, Juliet says, unless you're applying to be a standup comedian, Juliet's mother says, checkmate, Juliet says, you could have made that move yesterday why did you wait till tonight, Juliet's mother says, bedtime, Juliet says, what are you my mother, Juliet's mother says, yes mother, Juliet says, recommendation.equals.hire, Juliet's mother says, you're snoring already are you asleep or, Juliet's mother says, the paper boats won't float for long unless you fold them with the good carton, Antonio says, make no mistake, Antonio's sister says, it was a mistake to lose our family photos, lowering her voice to the dark caves under the earth she called Black Mole, Black Mole, Doctor Sueño reads, come out and make the sauce because Juan is going to eat the Angel, all night long, Lionel Richie says, who ordered the light switches, the lanky student says, they handcuffed him and he tried to raise his head from the floor to see if anyone was going to help him, Juliet says, who was trying to raise his head, Juliet's mother says, did you just wake up too, Juliet says, synchronized as usual, Juliet's mother says, past midnight, Juliet says, the earth might be uninhabited, Juliet's mother says, I wish this synchronization of ours included you not taking all the covers I'm freezing, Juliet says, I cold you because I love you, Juliet's mother says, I burr you because I what's a word with double Rs, Juliet says, go on what have you dreamed so far, Juliet's mother says, Doctor Sueño was reading me a story about a Black Mole who lived in the dark caves under the earth, Juliet says, Doctor Sueño being the original implant, Juliet's mother says, should we search Black Mole + dark caves to see if it's a dream someone wrote down already or, Juliet says, what do you think the dream means, Juliet's mother says, let me dream on it, Juliet says, see you in like two hours, Juliet's mother says, all night long, Juliet says, lowering her voice to the dark caves under the earth she called Black Mole, Black Mole, Antonio's sister reads, come out and make the sauce because Juan is going to eat the Angel.

Ada's Father

Dear humans, Ada's father says, I grew up with a family of roly polys, my parents left me to fight in the anteater war and never came back, I don't want to hear this right now, Ada says, instructing Leonora to skip the recording of his father reading a story she'd written for a school competition when she was ten years old (when she was a sophomore at Yale her father had sent her the photos he'd taken of that story along with a message explaining why he was sending her this recording of her story — isn't it amusing that I know you want to talk to me, her father wrote, and of course I want to talk to you, but we end up not talking very often because what is there to say? — you don't want to tell me about your boring day, Ada wrote, and because I inherited your sparkling introversion I also don't want to tell you or anyone else about my boring day — right and yet while the day is happening, her father wrote, I'm always either narrating it to you or having a conversation with you in my head — that sounds too melodramatic, Ada wrote — you are correct, her father wrote, these imaginary conversations and / or narrations don't happen every day, and when they do happen they don't happen all throughout the day, and so I wonder if I have come to assume you're one of my omniscient narrators, always watching me, the other narrators being my mother, your mother, the Virgin Mary, my Catholic high school idea of god, in others words perhaps I don't feel like telling you about my day not only because the telling would be boring but because I assume you already know about my day since you were there, watching it unfold —), my new family is really, um, how do I put this, strange, Ada's father says, did I imagine I said skip this track or are you low on batteries, Ada says, that's not a track that's your father reading a story of yours, Leonora Carrington says, let me just make one thing clear, Ada's father says, I'm this tall, that's right, Ada (as her father) says, I'm the shortest one in your grade, maybe in the whole school, maybe in the whole world, and as Ada instructs Leonora to call her sister again, an enforcement patrol approaches her on the Bay Bridge, staying level with her, and as the officer on the passenger side assesses her with what looks like a periscope on his hand and apparently clears her because the patrol car is speeding away, and as her sister in Bogotá continues to not answer her phone, Leonora continues to not skip her roly poly story as read by her father, a story she'd shared with him when she was ten years old and they were driving to City Lights Books and she said can I read you a story I wrote, Tata, of course is it about when I first met your mother while she was selling mangoes on the side of the road, her father said, can I read it to you now, Ada said, anytime except when I am asleep am I asleep watch out your driver's asleep, her father said, this letter took me three years to write, Ada read, and the reason I wrote this three year letter is because I need your help, Ada's father says, a family of grasshoppers has attacked my home, Ada read, my roly poly sister has been killed and our house burned, Ada says, in fact a bunch of human kids have been taking my roly poly family away and all that is left is me, alone, her father says, I lived in a house across the street from a huge school, Ada read, now I live in a huge forest with a big tree in the middle — do you want me to comment on your story? — who is this? — I know you know who this is — too late the story already didn't win — press rewind — rewind — say urraca — urraca — okay you're cured you can stop crying now — after going over what I wrote to you yesterday, her father wrote, I would like to clarify that my cadre of omniscient narrators doesn't always convene to watch me, in other words sometimes only the Virgin Mary shows up, sometimes you and your mother show up, and so on — dear feather, Ada wrote, I found you floating on the sidewalk but couldn't find your bird host, and yet instead of powering up my narrative machine and launching a narrative about Ada searching for your bird host, facing obstacles constructed out of bricks and elaborate sentences, discovering Ada shouldn't have skipped class to search for your bird host because now she'll be stuck in after school detention for years, which isn't much of a story, The End, I attached you to my coat's sleeve so as to feel lighter — dear feather attacher, her father wrote, one day you will become a magpie and fly away toward me — dear feather, Ada wrote, do we, your cadre of omniscient narrators, talk to each other while the action is taking place? — enough, Ada says, stop roly poly story, your sentiment scores say otherwise are you sure, Leonora Carrington says, I'm not sure but I'm tired of hearing this story, Ada says, tired of the obvious parallels between my father's deportation and the narrator's parents leaving her to fight a stupid anteater war, I don't see any parallels you stayed here with your mother and your father returns to you in the form of him reading your roly poly story out loud, Doctor Sueño says, help me by giving me a new home, a tiny pencil, a notebook, Ada's father says, some tea, a tiny backpack and somebody to take care of me, the part about the bear, Ada says, I like that part too, Doctor Sueño says, when we get to class I get settled on a bookshelf next to a bear holding a heart, Ada's father says, I like the part about the narrator being studious, Doctor Sueño says, the only way I wrote this letter is because I pay attention in spelling and grammar class, Ada's father says, and when her father parked by City Lights Books, Ada was disappointed because she hadn't finished reading him her story yet, but her father didn't say enough let's go he said please continue I want to hear how your story ends, so they stayed inside that red German SUV he'd leased on a whim when his sister (and this Ada found out years later, when she'd asked him if his second novel about a sister that loses parts of her reason was autobiographical) had begun to lose parts of her reason, interrupted by an audience of cars peering inside his window to ascertain if they were leaving or parking or what — dear daughter number one, Ada's father wrote, I am sitting in a kitchen, different than the one you're in now, I am about to record the sound of my voice, again and again, until the, hold on, I forget how that Alvin Lucier piece goes let me ask daughter number two in any case we're in the kitchen and we're projecting the photos of your story on the wall and I am going to record me reading it to you so that, every time I think of you, I can avoid the mental sequence of (1) should I call daughter (2) even though I have (3) nothing to say, and instead send you a two letter message, rp for roly poly, maybe even add a number to indicate where to start the recording of rp, you know, for variety's sake — dear father of daughters one and two, Ada wrote, why don't you, for variety's sake, send me recordings of you reading multiple stories simultaneously, like It's Going to Rain by Steve Reich but with you as multiple street preachers — when Mozart was composing his music he would hear the entirety of a piece all at once, Doctor Sueño says, as if time didn't progress but was a lake that already contained all his music — we're going to video conference you while we project your story on the wall please hold, Ada's father wrote — what do you see can you see, Ada's father says, I don't want to intrude on the recording are you already recording, Ada says, you'll find out when I send it to you, Ada's father says, a tiny pencil, Ada read by City Lights Books, a notebook, some tea, a tiny backpack and somebody to take care of me, I had in mind this girl [photo of Ada], Ada (as her father) says, put all my things in here [pouch attached to page], thank you for reading this I hope we meet soon and overcome the attacks sent by the grasshoppers, Ada's father says, but what if I'm like Mozart, Ada thinks, and my contents exist all together inside a lake: (1) the black unmarked sedans with tinted windows streaming on the Bay Bridge, (1) a drawing of me smiling next to the word Lilttutobpg, (1) the video of my video by Doctor Sueño that removed all the original images and replaced them with images of missing houses, (1) the evening at a narrow church when I heard Edward Hirsch read about a substitute teacher who said rhinos have poor eyesight and swivel their tube shaped ears in all directions so they can hear their enemies approaching, (1) the evening my father said I will buy you Coca-Cola and ice cream if you come with me to this concert at Grace Cathedral, where a man shrouded in purple robes appeared from behind the stage and recited a poem from a piece of paper, a poem that consisted of vowel sounds, as if he was trying to test the reverberations of the church, proceeding to smash the piano for the next hour, and her father said why don't you draw whatever comes to mind while you're listening to this music, and so she did, drawing spirals with faces on the church's envelopes for donations, and later her father collected them and framed them, what's that called, Eva said, Cecil Taylor by Ada Rodriguez, her father said, don't take him, Ada says, shut up we have a removal order for him, the American abductor says, an abductor who was wearing a vest with the word Police on its back, you are not police you are nothing, Ada says, we are the nothing that counts, the fake policeman says, isn't that wonderful?

Interpretations

Flying saucers surround our neighborhood, Amparo Dávila says, searching for The Implanted, when did you realize you were dreaming, Doctor Sueño says, when I heard the sound of the flying saucers like that of helicopters at quadruple the speed, Amparo Dávila says, what did you modify while lucid dreaming, Doctor Sueño says, I would rather know what she should have modified, Auxilio Lacouture says, I would have flown away atop one of the saucers, Remedios Varo says, you mean you would have written a letter to the aliens saying greetings I'm a Peruvian alpinist I need your alien rope to climb away from here, Auxilio Lacouture says, if you fly away you are leaving behind The Implanted to be suctioned into the flying saucers, Amparo Dávila says, so what I don't know them I've never received potted plants from them, Auxilio Lacouture says, antihumanist interpretations are welcome because they broaden the possibilities of our humanity, etc., Doctor Sueño says, I would have willed laser guns into existence to overcome the flying saucers and extirpate everyone's implants, Remedios Varo says, the lucid good Samaritan how boring can we press fast forward, Amparo Dávila says, what did you modify while lucid dreaming, Doctor Sueño says, I stood still, terrified, Amparo Dávila says, watching The Implanted being suctioned into the flying saucers, everything in your dream is you, Auxilio Lacouture says, we're not doing that today, Doctor Sueño says, can you lucid dream your way into the same dream scenario such that while you're standing still amid the flying saucers you're also dreaming that you're not standing still amid the flying saucers, Amparo Dávila says, we have us another caller you're on the air tell us your name and your dream, Doctor Sueño says, my name is Silvia but call me Silvina Ocampo so I can fit in with Amparo and Auxilio and Remedios I've had that same dream about the flying saucers though I think you might be disappointed with the literalness of my interpretation, Silvina Ocampo says, I'm sure it will be more amusing than anything from Remedios's dictionary, Amparo Dávila says, to dream you are referring to a boring dictionary signifies you will depend too much upon the boring opinion of others for the clean management of your own affairs, Remedios Varo says, after the American abductors wrenched my daughter from me they affixed a monitor on my right ankle, Silvina Ocampo says, and one night, unable to fall asleep yet again because what if my daughter was trying to contact me I know the three of you believe in telepathy, yes we already knew you were going to say I know the three of us believe in telepathy, Amparo Dávila says, one night I heard a beeping and I thought it must be the oven because I had just been dreaming of putting my head in the oven, Silvina Ocampo says, which wasn't an unpleasant dream because someone in the background kept saying her head smells like muffins, but as you probably already inferred given that I started by focusing on the ankle monitor the beeping originated from my ankle monitor I thought maybe the batteries were low but no that morning I had attached my ankle to the wall charger have you ever placed your ear against the wall of an apartment building and expected to hear the patter of raccoons or the voices of the other tenants, I thought maybe the man in the control tower has insomnia and is pressing buttons at random, or maybe the man in the control tower is trying to amuse himself by beeping Für Elise into everyone's ankles, which I am sorry to say wasn't the case though I listened attentively for that quaint tune just as I had listened attentively to the voices of the other tenants inside the wall so I thought maybe the insomniac American in the control tower knows where his compatriots have taken my daughter and he's beeping me my daughter's abduction location, which wasn't as improbable as some of your listeners might think even though I know your listeners prefer the improbable the reason it wasn't improbable was that my face had been on the news cycle poor Silvina Ocampo has escaped the barbarity of her home country and now has to endure the barbarity of this American country later I thought maybe my seventeen month old daughter escaped and has taken over the control tower here's where our doctor should say even the most preposterous possibilities will navigate across the sea of your mind later I thought maybe the American abductors were coming for me and the beeping was a simple latitude / longitude calculation though as you probably know you don't need a beeping sound to calculate anything can you imagine the computer programmer who was asked by his boss to pick the beeping sound of the ankle monitors make it ominous like the alarm of a toy truck because the beeping started at around 2:00 AM I worried about the neighbors complaining about my alarmed ankle I thought of the American professor who had allowed me to stay in one of his apartments for three weeks at most receiving a message from the building manager we've been informed of an alien alarm sound originating from your apartment p.s. we didn't know you collected toy trucks the professor sending me a message I am sorry to inform you due to noise complaints I am going to have to ask you to leave I hope you understand I don't own that apartment I rent it I don't want any trouble later during dinner the professor telling his wife and his well behaved kids that ungrateful refugee made such a ruckus at night that the neighbors complained I had to apologize and explain that it wasn't me so to avoid ruining the professor's dinner I wrapped a blanket around my ankle monitor to minimalize my alarmed ankle I thought don't switch on any lights Silvia I mean Silvina but do make your way to the kitchen where the alien alarm would have less of an impact on the neighbors unless the neighbors are awake and boiling themselves some meth soup ha ha on my way to the kitchen with the blanket tied to my ankle I thought of toilet paper I thought at last I have a tail I thought at last I own a theatrical wedding dress but no one laughed I thought maybe I should whisper my coordinates to the ankle monitor so that it would cease its alarm maybe it was the ankle monitor's alarm clock time to wake up and go to work but no one laughed at the image of the ankle monitor putting on its hat and going to work I was still half asleep I thought I was dreaming the drone tapping on the window in the kitchen merely this and nothing more so I opened the window and the drone came inside and stared at me first from one side then from another side please refrain from any cubist jokes until the end of this interpretation I said do you want some chamomile tea the drone said nothing I said good because I don't know what kind of tea the professor has in his cabinets or whether I am allowed to drown his tea bags the drone said nothing here I want to clarify that I wasn't dreaming and that although now it isn't unreasonable to expect a drone to contain chatbots or a transmission of a speaking human, back then drones didn't speak yet and so either I was already living in the future or I was confused about whether I was living in the present or the future so I sat down in the one chair in the kitchen of the American professor and the not yet with voice drone positioned itself in front of me, three or five steps away from me, slightly above my head I thought whosoever sent this mute drone wants me to know his machine is a kind of Jehovah, watching me from above, I thought Jehovah the Drone will slice my throat with its blades and transmit my death live with its videocamera which back then drones did have but maybe its videocamera doesn't come with flash so as long as I don't switch on the lights I am safe but what's going to happen when the sun recurs of course I didn't want to make any sudden moves even though the drone wasn't a bear or a snake or a crocodile or whatever animal one isn't supposed to make sudden moves when encountered of course I was scared but of course humans can get used to anything so after a while of nothing happening I got used to the sound of this Jehovah drone like a plague of locusts at quadruple the speed I thought perhaps an American from Kansas or Ohio or Montana or Oregon called his cousin at the ankle monitor company and said cousin where is my meth soup ha ha cousin I saw on the news some mongrel from Central America is whining about our government kidnapping her seventeen month old daughter here's my credit card number I want to buy the bestest premium surveillance ankle monitor package and the cousin said I will give you the three month premium special which comes with a drone I will give you access to the drone feed so you can keep an eye on the mongrel yourself I thought I am falling asleep I said bedtime, cousin, I thought if they can keep track of me with a drone they can keep track of my daughter, which as we all know now wasn't the case, I am disappointed none of you have asked me if my head really smells like muffins I thought Auxilio or Amparo or Remedios were going to ask me about that but here we are I am almost done with my dream interpretation and no one has said anything, I remember you, Auxilio Lacouture says, you and your daughter at the San Francisco airport, Amparo Dávila says, your daughter Juliet how is she, Remedios Varo says, I thought this was a dream interpretation show not a crying show, Silvina Ocampo says, we apologize for the technical difficulties, Doctor Sueño says, goddamn it, Silvina Ocampo says, this happens to me every time.

Juliet's Mother

On the other hand she has always been able to recognize that resentful creature as herself, Juliet thinks as she watches a video entitled Witness a Mother's Call with her Daughter in Government Custody, a video that begins with ominous music and a black screen that explains that American abductors separated a toddler named Juliet from her mother and that Juliet is in the custody of a government contracted shelter, you're upset at me, Juliet's mother says, she hasn't gotten sick, one of the American accomplices says, soon you will be with me, Juliet's mother says, but Juliet avoids the source of her mother's voice in a video she shouldn't be watching at work for more than ten seconds or the algorithms will subtract from her Focus Score so she closes the video of herself not looking at her mother, continues to code until her alarm signals the end of five minutes (one of the men in charge of the monitoring algorithms (Salvador or Labrador or whatever his name is) tried to impress her by sharing with her that if video streaming >= 10 seconds, then subtract 0.05% from Focus Score, do until 5 minutes), launches the video again at 0:10 and inside her headphones Juliet mother's says Juliet, Juliet, not pleading with her yet — please look at me, Juliet — never again, mother — but as if trying to wake her, too gently, though, as if she's concerned she might startle Juliet's out of her dreamscape — what do you even know about my dreamscape? — you tell me about it every night? — okay besides that — your voice hasn't changed, mother, Juliet says, but in that video Juliet doesn't reply, Juliet, Juliet's mother says, Juliet, how many Juliets does it take for a Juliet to acknowledge a mother, Juliet says, but the seventeen month old version of Juliet, the one who's sitting on a file cabinet next to a screen showcasing trailers of cartoon movies inside an empty room which over the years has looked to her like an antechamber for fax machines — please wait here while we retrieve your fax machine from storage, ma'am — or like the stage setting for a corporate take on No Exit, which she once saw with her mother at Teatro La Concha (she doesn't remember a word from that play but she does remember her mother being the only one in the audience that laughed throughout, as if she had been hired to confuse the audience about what the play was about), doesn't look toward the device that's transmitting her mother's voice, your ten seconds are up, an intraoffice immediate message from Salvador says, rewind my seconds or I will reply with the word cr**p and you'll be in trouble with employer relations too ha ha, Juliet types, I deactivated all keyword triggers before messaging you, Salvador types, smart creep, Juliet types, I don't belong here, Salvador types, emo creep how many minus points for singing, Juliet types, don't worry I can't see what you're watching I can only see the metadata that says you're watching a video on an American news site see you later maybe, Salvador types, hopefully not, Juliet types, and hopefully no one can see the video that she's been watching, Juliet thinks, although why should she care if anyone does (if she had to explain herself in front of a Focus Score committee, Juliet would declare that many years ago, esteemed cr**ps, I promised myself I would not watch these videos of me anymore, and for the most part I have kept to my promise (yes, I know this keeping of promises business sounds too much like the language of elementary school but you didn't give me enough time to prepare my speech), and yet unfortunately an obscure novelist from Colombia interviewed me yesterday about those videos and here I am again, watching how that resentful creature doesn't look at her mother again and cries at the sound of her mother's voice, and what you probably don't care to know is that I have already imagined this moment, many years ago I already saw myself watching these videos again and not watching these videos again due to a global outage that purged these videos forever), you're upset at me, Juliet's mother says, yes I am upset at you you let those horrible people take me away from you, Juliet says, keep your horrible voice down, one of Juliet's coworker says, that's at least a 0.005% subtraction, Juliet says, the algorithms have been updated to recognize my play on words, Ju-late, Juliet's coworker says, Juliet has become attached to the head of the shelter, one of the American accomplices says as a woman whose face has been blurred holds Juliet, who has been crying on the shoulder of this blurred woman as her mother says Juliet, Juliet, yes, Juliet thinks, no matter how much she has tried to rationalize her separation from her mother (my mother didn't want the American abductors to separate us, Juliet wrote many years ago in a journal she entitled Mom & I, my mother couldn't stop them from separating us, my mother wanted me back, my mother spoke to journalists and allowed them to film her daughter in detention so as to force the American abductors to reunite her with her daughter), no matter how many expunge the past therapies she undergoes (she has already tried constellation therapy, rebirthing, gestalt, and last year her mother convinced her to try a more traditional talk therapy approach together, but as soon as the therapist said what brings you here her mother sobbed and there wasn't anything the therapist could say to bring her back — where do you go when you sob, mother? — a cave, a tunnel, an abandoned cathedral where obsolete hymns continue to reverberate — and the therapist seemed surprised Juliet wasn't trying to console her mother, as if her mother's sobbing was Juliet's fault, shrugging as if to say how is this my fault, doctor — I know I am the source of her despair, Juliet wrote, but if I say I am sorry when I am not, wouldn't that just increase this intractable resentment I feel toward her?), she still, after all these years (and here Juliet thinks of subterranean passageways where her resentment circulates like blood inside her veins — I detest the word resentment, Juliet wrote, because it sounds too resentful? — what do you want to call it instead? — subterranean rancor? interplanetary indignation? — by which she doesn't mean that she doesn't bring flowers to her mother at least once a week (from the same makeshift flower shop next to a coffee cart that consists of a robot's arm that prepares your cortados and streams Frank Sinatra songs as if to make the robot's arm more relatable — I prefer the versions were the lyrics of these Sinatra songs have been scrambled, the flower lady once said — why isn't this chain of robot coffee carts called The Claw? —), or that she doesn't brush her mother's hair at least once a month (when she was little her mother would ask her to pluck her silver hairs, but by the time she was in high school her mother's hair was at least 2/3 silver so that enterprise was abandoned by mutual agreement (when she was in high school she dreamt of fax machines, which didn't make any sense — if you dream of fax machines you will receive a fax in the near or distant future, Remedios Varo says — and when later she watched those videos of herself again she associated the empty room for fax machines in the dream with the empty room where she wasn't looking toward where her mother was saying Juliet, Juliet (at some point in the video whoever's holding the device transmitting her mother's voice turns around and the viewer can see an empty room with a red leather couch that she didn't notice the first time she watched the video, a red leather couch she should have dreamt about instead of those stupid fax machines (the fax machines weren't even in the dream she just knew the empty room was for fax machines) except while she was watching No Exit with her mother she remembers thinking she would rather be watching a play about a red leather couch that looked as if it had been discarded by a line dancing nightclub in Texas but on their way to their daily abductions the American abductors spotted it on the sidewalk and brought it back to the room as a joke — American Abductor #1: I bet your mom wears lipstick as electric as this couch — American Abductor #2: at least my mom doesn't look like a couch — American Abductor #3: why does American Abductor #2 always get the best lines? — American Abductor #4: his mom can't look like a couch because she's dead — American Abductors #1-4: thank you we'll be here all week —)), or that tonight she won't embrace her mother at least twice before going to bed and say I've missed you today, and her mother will probably say is this you or the implant talking, and Juliet will probably say that I've automated my missing statement doesn't diminish the intent of my missing statement, and her mother will probably say what missing statement what am I missing, and Juliet will probably say fine the statement of missingnessness, and her mother will probably say did you sign up for that holotropic breathwork therapy I told you about, and Juliet will probably say yes mother but I am going to this one alone, and after her day's work is done, after elevator, sidewalk, subway, sidewalk, Juliet opens the door of her house and her mother says that dream you had last night is from a painter, what dream what painter, Juliet says, the one about the black mole here I wrote it down, Juliet's mother says, you write down my dreams, Juliet says, yes they're for a book called Juliet's Dreams as Explained by Her Mother, Juliet's mother says, what does the dream mean, Juliet says, I was going to write a letter to the painter asking what her black mole dream meant but she's dead ha ha, Juliet's mother says, call Doctor Sueño he'll know, Juliet says), resents that woman in the video who says Juliet, Juliet, soon we'll be together again.

Unimaginable

I can't imagine the conditions either, Antonio thinks, every time he has tried he has failed to imagine the conditions that would force him and his daughters to flee San Francisco and request asylum in a different country (he hasn't tried to imagine the conditions very often because why would he want to?), although he's been able to imagine himself rising toward a place from where the conditions would be just about visible but then hitting a glass dome that blurs what's going on on the other side, no, Antonio says to his daughters during dinner, Americans can't imagine the conditions, and if they can't imagine the conditions, they can't imagine themselves as refugees, and if they can't imagine themselves as refugees, they will conclude that refugees are different from them, a different species, Eva says, they read in the news that a different species from Central America have to flee their homes and that they're coming here, asking for our help, and that we're telling them we don't want them here, and that we're abducting their children to teach them a lesson, life is hard and then we die, Ada says, don't say that out loud you know your mother doesn't, Antonio says, I say it out loud at school that's why I'm a friendless child ha ha, Ada says, the refrain either way we're all going to die is supposed to be an affirmation of life, Antonio says, what are you three whispering about, Antonio's former wife says, firmaments of life, Eva says, but Americans don't sit down to write dear diary today I have concluded that refugees are a different species than me, no, Antonio says, if you ask Americans if they believe refugees are a different species than them they will not only say absolutely not but they will lodge a complaint to the management saying you have offended them, can I speak to the manager my father is an affront to the American people, Ada says, affront's a good word where did you read it, Antonio says, affront rhymes with sasquatch, Eva says, no it doesn't, Ada says, are we Americans, Eva says, yes but your mother is from Czechia and your father is from Colombia, Antonio says, so we're not Americans, Ada says, the four of us are American citizens, Antonio says, but because your parents didn't grow up here the false narratives of the United States being the best country in the world or a beacon of light incapable of wrongdoing aren't part of our consciousness, or at least not as much as for those who have grown up here, so even if these refugees were blonde Canadians you think Americans wouldn't care about them, Antonio's former wife says, bigotry is definitely one of the glass domes, Antonio says, but even if you manage to cross that dome you would still encounter the other one, the one about different species, Ada says, excessive misfortune changes the American system of classification, Antonio says, our system of classification, Ada says, did anyone dream last night, Antonio says, my dreams are an affront to the imagination of the American people, Ada says, I dreamed that you stopped leaving your dirty shorts in the living room, Antonio's former wife says, everyone in your dream is you according to Doctor Sueño, Antonio says, uhhh Tata just called Mama dirty shorts, Ada says, the zombie apocalypse is coming but we can't buy the right guns, Eva says, so we order them online and wait, I told you not to read to them from that zombie book, Antonio's former wife says, they're not zombies they're the undead, Ada says, hey Sisyphus read the first line of A Questionable Shape by Bennett Sims, Antonio says, that's not how phones work, Tata, Eva says, what we know about the undead so far is this, Antonio (as Sisyphus) reads, they.return.to.familiar. places, but when Antonio (as Antonio) has tried to imagine the unfamiliar conditions that would force him and his daughters to flee San Francisco and request asylum in a different country, Antonio thinks, he hasn't been able to do it either, come back to earth, Tato, Antonio's former wife says, my classmates say Americans faked the moon landing, Ada says, everyone wash your own plate and go finish your homework, Antonio's former wife says, my math homework is an affront to faerie handbags everywhere, Ada says, but perhaps if I write down the conditions as simple formulas, Antonio thinks, if X then Y, Antonio writes, where X equals bank accounts are frozen due to being Latin American and Y equals a plane ride to Czechia, fine, but he could just transfer the ownership of his accounts to his former wife, who isn't Latin American, can you check my math homework when you're done, Eva says, anytime, bunnytown, Antonio says, if X then Y, Antonio writes, where X equals being barred from working in the United States for being Latin American and Y equals a plane ride to Czechia, but even if he isn't allowed to work his former wife could work as a kindergarten teacher, which, sure, would mean they would have to move to a smaller apartment far away from

San Francisco, and he would have to let go of his studio apartment and move in with his former wife and his daughters again, so if X equals solvable condition and Y equals bearable escape option, Antonio thinks, then his if statement equals ludicrous because he has read the reports about Central American refugees escaping the most harrowing X conditions (extortion, death threats, rape, kidnappings, murder) via the most unbearable Y escape options (a dangerous ride atop a train swarmed by kidnappers, a river crossing, a desert where bands of angry Pale Americans have organized themselves to make sure there's not even water available for these refugees) so he knows he just doesn't want to transpose these harrowing conditions and these unbearable escape options to his family, can I tell you my dream from last night, Ada says, of course let me switch on the recorder, Antonio says, I am wearing a white suit for a wedding and I have Eva's mouse in my pocket, Ada says, which I present to the bride as a gift, but we haven't even gotten Eva's mouse yet, Antonio's former wife says, please tell me Eva's joking about getting a pet mouse, Antonio says, someone is at the door, Antonio's former wife says, are we expecting anyone, Antonio says, probably a late delivery I'll get it, Antonio's former wife says, no don't open the door, Antonio says, who's there, Antonio's former wife says, I'm here to repair your sink, someone says, we didn't ask for our sink to be repaired, Antonio's former wife says, don't open the door, Antonio says, just need to take a quick look, someone else says, are they wearing bullet proof vests how many of them are there, Antonio says, don't be so paranoid, Antonio's former wife says, I am not kidding don't open the door, Antonio says, I can't see them it's dark outside, Antonio's former wife says, who sent you, Antonio says, building manager, one of them says, what's his name,

Antonio says, is this apartment eight, the other one says, apartment two, Antonio says, what is happening, Eva says, wrong apartment sorry, one of them says, what is happening, Ada says, wrong number, Antonio says.

Eva's Father

Not Ada's video, Eva thinks, not even once, no, not even after some of her concerned classmates informed her that Ada's video was amassing thousands of views around the world, as if she should have cared about this embarrassing tide of murmurs rising in her direction, nor did she watch Ada's video after the rest of her classmates in her elementary school, the ones who already resented her for ridiculing their mindless obsession with the right kind of coloring pencils in #relatable, her monthly cartoon, which was rejected by the school's newspaper that month because it was too mean but which she circulated among her classmates during recess anyhow, badgered her about her father being a criminal who shouldn't have been in the United States to begin with, and perhaps she avoided Ada's video not only for the obvious reason of why watch it if she'd been there and once was enough for her but because she'd been worried she might be expelled from school because of it, in other words she had come to believe, with the spurious rationale of an eight year old who, against her father's wishes, was beginning to enjoy the cosmos of Christ that was being inculcated to her by teachers who pretended they were not inculcating Christ but just sharing him — your father doesn't have to be a believer to be part of our community, Eva — that if she watched Ada's video (or was forced to watch Ada's video in an interrogation room, as she had often imagined throughout the years), she would ruin her chances of negating the contents of Ada's video and would therefore increase the chances of being expelled on the grounds that her father must be a criminal if, as shown in Ada's video, three policemen who weren't policemen apprehended him in front of his daughters — why did you apprehend my father on the our way to school? couldn't you have waited for him to at least drop us off? — who is this? — in other words if she didn't watch Ada's video, Eva believed back then (and probably still believes even now, next to the medical equipment inputting breaths into his father at the Hospital Luis Vernaza, because beliefs from childhood are like those phosphorescent serums that circumnavigate our veins in search of (what?) an outlet — installation idea, Eva writes, audience members on foldable chairs inside an empty warehouse / nurses inject them with phosphorescent serum / machines track the course of their serums which will be amplified on an immense screen / hundreds of phosphorescent pathways on an immense screen / like a Jackson Pollock everyone will say / no like a live piece by Tristan Perich —), in other words if she didn't watch Ada's video, if she didn't allow those images to become part of who she was to become but instead allowed them to be submerged in a pond beneath a cave far away from here (installation idea, Eva thinks but doesn't write anything since nothing comes to mind besides an image of a pond and an image of electrodes on her brain), that would have increased the chances that what unfolded in Ada's video didn't happen and therefore that it wasn't even remotely possible that her father was a criminal, but perhaps she didn't watch Ada's video because she had intuited that Ada's video might be interpreted as a bad omen, given that teachers, parents, and students watching Ada's video would recognize, in the background, half a block from her school, the convenience store where most of the students bought potato chips after school and their parents bought fresh bagels before school, the same convenience store that had caused a stir among the parents of three fifth graders who had been caught by a teacher being offensive to the young Pakistani man behind the counter, a young Pakistani man who had dismissed the incident as nothing at all, which is the opposite of what the parents of the three fifth graders did — our children would have never behave like that that teacher must have misunderstood she's not even from here — your father isn't a criminal, the principal said, I know that, Eva said, he has done nothing wrong, the principal said, I already know that, Ada said, and unfortunately Ada's video had been a bad omen as she'd feared because less than a year after the American abductors abducted her father — it is so tiring to continue to house you here after all these years get out of here already — we're here for you, alien — whine in English ha ha — leave her alone can't you see her father is dying? — octopuses don't die they drip ink get it? — the American abductors escalated their abductions, reactivating a sequence that humans have been rehearsing for thousands of years: (i) a limited number of people are abducted (three of her classmates, all Latin American, which, and this she has never told anyone, didn't matter much to her because she didn't play with any of them, doesn't even remember their names, plus Miss Viola could pay more attention to her since there were three less kids to worry about), (ii) limited protective measures are taken (her mother changes Ada and Eva's last name from her father's (Rodriguez) to hers (Brzeszczykowski)), (iii) a not so limited number of people are abducted (six more classmates, all Latin American), (iv) those implicated but not targeted transport their families elsewhere (the only two Pale American classmates of hers transfer to Urbania, a non-Catholic private school, their parents, according to her mother, citing the need for their children to avoid the trauma of their classmates' disappearances, plus Urbania has a great theater program — the curtains, Maria! —), (v) additional protective measures are taken (Ada and Eva stand in front of the bathroom mirror, staring at their new blonde hair — you look like a rabbit — you mean we? —), (vi) the abductors attempt to meet their performance targets by whatever means necessary (the American abductors barge into her school, demand a list of all the students, handcuff the principal, who refuses to hand over anything, intimidate the vice principal into handing over everything, barge into each classroom, call out the names of the kids with a Latin American last name, plus those who look Latin American, line them up in the patio, as if they are about to ask the kids to pledge to the flag or sing the national anthem, crack jokes about something Eva can't hear — que le dijo un guante a otro guante? — que? — I glove you — wait for the vans to arrive, load them into the vans, The End), installation idea, Eva said to her father over the phone too many years ago, when she was still a freshman at Yale, the audience sits on empty school desks in what resembles the patio of an elementary school, love it, Eva's father said, you don't love it I can see it in your face, Eva said, how can you see my face from over there, Eva's father said, telepathic reconstructive reimaging, Eva said, I do love it but perhaps, Eva's father said, perhaps what, Eva said, I don't think you need my opinion you're already, Eva's father said, out with it, fa-fa-father, Eva said, perhaps the empty desks are a seed, Eva's father said, a clue to a potential installation, not the installation itself, try, for instance, to isolate the moment at your elementary school when you were most terrified because that kind of moment, in my experience, often contains what will allow you to cross to where you'll find the Gremlins you are after, Gremlins already exist in their own movies so that's not making it new, Eva said, good one, Eva's father said, neither good nor bad señor, Eva said, but okay the moment I was most terrified was when the American abductors barged into my classroom, first or second floor, Eva's father said, second, Eva said, did you hear them tramping up the stairs, Eva's father said, no but over the years I've imagined them climbing hundreds of stairs to apprehend me, Eva said, and I remember as soon as they barged into my classroom I was sure they were searching for Ada and I because of everything we'd said about them in those angry rallies seeking your release from detention, and I remember concentrating on Miss Viola's face to ascertain whether the situation was really as bad as I thought (it was), and when they started calling out names I couldn't hear what they were saying, as if my nervous system had shut down my hearing to shield me, Lola Martinez, one of the abductors said, her name too familiar for my shield to function properly, and I can still see myself standing up and shouting don't take my best friend but of course I didn't stand up, didn't shout anything, and I remember the sound of backpacks and coats being released from their hooks and one of the American abductors saying nope, no room for backpacks today, as if they had come some other day there might have been room for backpacks just not today, sorry, those are some terrifying moments for an eight year old to live through, Eva's father said, what are you my therapist, Eva said, you are getting very sleepy the collective unconscious is about to take your call, Eva's father said, and I remember trying to calm down by repeating what you'd told me, Eva said, the worst that can happen is that you come to live with Tata, Eva's father said, which wasn't true, Eva said, and I remember wondering if these men were scattered all over our school already and whether Ada was repeating the same false mantra of deportation at the same time, and I remember the men staring at me as if trying to discern whether I was Latin American, and when it was over the electric current inside my arms didn't switch off, if the current is still on can you power my reading lamp please, Eva's father said, not funny, Eva said, forgive me, Eva's father said, and I remember being too scared to approach the windows like everyone else but I eventually did, what caught your attention down in the patio, Eva's father said, right so once I had confirmed Ada wasn't there I remember thinking it was odd that one of the American abductors had carried a desk and a chair from one of the classrooms out to the patio, as if he was about to sit down behind the desk and hand out report cards or paychecks, but no, he sat down and pulled a notepad from the side pocket of his cargo pants and started writing on it, as if he was taking notes for his memoir about that time when he rounded up those goddamn Latinos and ejected them from the United States of America, and I remember thinking the vans were taking too long because the teacher tried to resume the class and we could still hear them milling out there, not as if they were at recess, no, like a silent pantomime of recess, and I remember telling myself it's probably not so bad since most of them had already been told by their parents about the possibility of the American abductors showing up at our school — we would never enter sensitive locations like churches or schools ha ha whatever — perhaps some of them were relieved that at last the moment they'd feared had come, Eva's father said, and years later I remember wondering if the American abductors hadn't planned this operation ahead of time but had found themselves walking back from buying fresh bagels at the corner store and one of them had said my cousin so and so told me only Latinos attend these Catholic schools anymore let's go inside and catch a few of these mongrels, and to this day I sometimes think I could hear the sound of cars racing toward our school, parents, grandparents, cousins rushing toward us to say goodbye, to bring their kids blankets, Eva's father said, some of my classmates' backpacks already had blankets stashed in them since everyone had already heard about how those detention centers were like freezers, Eva said, you have plenty of terrifying moments to choose from, Eva's father said, I had forgotten that before the American abductors barged into my classroom I heard Ms. Jackie in the classroom next to ours screaming, Eva said, what did she scream did she say anything, Eva's father said, no she just screamed, Eva said, as if she had arrived at the part of the story she was reading to the first graders where the crocodiles eat the protagonist and was overdramatizing the being eaten part, so rare to hear unfettered screams which despite being rare are too familiar to us, Eva's father said, not so rare to hear unfettered sobs, Eva said, pick your moment, Eva's father said, do I have to pick just one, Eva said, remember that Borges story about the guy who is about to be shot and he asks god to give him more time and that moment in front of the firing squad goes on for years, Eva's father said, oh so you mean focus on that moment when the American abductors barged into my classroom and didn't call out my name because my mother had already changed our last names but I wasn't sure if she had, Eva said, eso mismo, Eva's father said, that would be for your installation not for mine my first installation has to be different than yours, Eva said, installation idea, Eva writes, equip audience with electrodes on brain / ask them to share favorite memory of childhood / submerge them in a replica of a pond / project blurry videos from a stock library of childhood memories pretend they're projections from their brains, don't forget to provide them with scuba diving equipment, Eva's father says, oh so you're awake, Eva says, I wrote about a pond once, Eva's father says, floaters deflate sir, Eva says, read that Borges story to me please, Eva's father says, that's not in your deathbed requirements, sir, Eva says, I am hereby amending my deathbed requirements, Eva's father says, I still remember when you read me that Leonora Carrington story about the face eating hyena, Eva says, yes we were at a parklet in Noe Valley waiting for your mother and Ada outside a hardware store that also sold toys, Eva's father says, The Secret Miracle by Jorge Luis Borges, Eva says to her watch Taryn Simon, and god caused him to die for a hundred years, Taryn Simon says, no I'll read it just project the text on the wall, Taryn Simon, Eva says, and so Eva reads out loud from The Secret Miracle, which begins with a dream by Hladik, the protagonist, a dream about a chess game that has been going on for centuries, what's the meaning of the dream, Eva's father says, as you well know, sir, Eva says, Borges despised psychological impulses so the dream has no psychological interpretation but it does set the stage for time as this vast, infinite place, skip the part about the Third Reich apprehending him and read Hladik's inner monologue while he's in captivity, Eva's father says, he inferred, Eva reads, with perverse logic, that to foresee any particular detail is in fact to prevent its happening, Eva reads, that's the opposite of what I think most of us think, Eva's father says, although of course how would I know what most of us think, that to foresee any particular detail is in fact to increase the chances of its happening, Eva says, right and I wonder if my mind has been secretly trying to counter Borges all these years since I read that story during my senior year at Yale, Eva's father says, he mused that the nights he slept were deep dim pools into which he could sink, Eva reads, sometimes, impatiently, Eva reads, he yearned for the shots that would end his life once and for all, isn't it silly that Hladik asks god to stop time so he can finish his incoherent play, Eva's father says, the play doesn't even take place it's happening in the character's mind the whole time, Eva says, I still love the part where god grants him his wish while he's in front of the firing squad, Eva's father says, yeah and the stoppage last years but really only two minutes, Eva says, add to those two minutes all those years since my senior year at Yale that I've carried Hladik's stoppage in front of the firing squad in my mind, two minutes divided by infinity plus fifty four years, let's end this farce / life with my favorite line, Eva's father says, no let's chat for a little while longer please, Eva says, Taryn Simon say my favorite line from The Secret Miracle, Eva's father says, Taryn Simon only responds to me, Eva says, not true I changed her settings before this death thing ha ha, Eva's father says, I will read it if you stop interrupting me, Taryn Simon says, go on sorry, Eva's father says, the physical world stopped and so on, Taryn Simon says.

Part V

Silvia's Son

I no longer mind that my son hates me, Silvia thinks, I don't know where my son is, Silvia says, when was the last time you, Eva says, do you have to record what I, Silvia says, to preserve your voice but I can, if you, Eva says, I don't want a capsule of time where I am always saying I no longer mind that my son hates me, Silvia says, because tomorrow I might mind again, Silvia thinks, if I listen to myself say I no longer mind that my son hates me I might obstruct the possibility of minding again why do I talk like this I am not an excessively self conscious person let's start over please don't expect me to be somber I am not a somber person either, what is your earliest memory of your son, Eva says, no one ever asks me about my son, Silvia says, the benevolent Americans assumed that because my son wasn't seized from me at the border, although they tried, Eva, I'd done my research before fleeing from Guatemala maybe research conjures the wrong images don't imagine me with reading glasses by an ancient desk in a musty room next to a pet rat eating the newspapers that were reporting that the American abductors at the border were tricking parents out of their children by saying things like I am going to take your son to get bathed don't worry I will bring him right back when a pleasant woman at the American detention center said to me I am taking your son to get bathed I screamed at her I said I know what you are trying to do the pleasant woman became unpleasant you don't scream at me I will have you placed in solitary confinement but she didn't come back that's when I noticed my son was trembling have you ever seen a human being tremble he was ten years old sometimes I think this is the moment he started to hate me but this isn't true the moment is a series of moments the moment I said to him we have to leave tonight he started to pack his drawings his comic books the portable cage for Roberto Carlos his pet rat my son was already an inward child he would leave the cage open for Roberto Carlos to climb on the curtains, jump on the bookshelf, land on his bed I had preserved the rat's journey on video I couldn't believe it but I had to say to him Esteban my love we can't bring any of our things I was a music teacher I had a baby grand piano at home Esteban would place Roberto Carlos atop the piano I think Roberto Carlos prefers Scriabin over Ravel he would say how do you know I would say I have been timing how long Roberto Carlos stays atop the piano he would say Roberto Carlos would scan me from left to right when I was playing that became our joke scanning each other like Roberto Carlos stupid things like this I remember you should write down Silvia is scanning Eva because the audio won't capture it, Silvia says, Juliet was with her father when she was taken from him, Eva says, you're doing it too you want to talk about Juliet instead of Esteban, Silvia says, I'm sorry I'm new at this sometimes my father would return from these interviews and say I have to be mindful of what they don't want to share I shouldn't press them but how does one know what anyone, Eva says, I don't remember what your father looked like but I remember the social worker saying his apartment reminded her of her college dorm room in Santa Cruz, Silvia says, I listened to the recording of his interview with Juliet he mentions you came to see his studio apartment we used to call that apartment The Other Home, Eva says, the other day I called into Doctor Sueño's transmission to explain my flying saucer dream when I was done sharing about how I lived in this American professor's apartment while I waited for news of Juliet I realized I hadn't mentioned Esteban, Silvia says, when was the last time you saw your son, Eva says, but Esteban was there by the time we arrived in San Francisco he didn't speak anymore he'd withdrawn completely after we left the professor's apartment he said I hid my coloring pencils in the professor's apartment what if he heard me on Doctor Sueño's transmission see I didn't exist for my mother then just as I don't exist for her now, wherever I am, Silvia says, where did he hide the coloring pencils, Eva says, he didn't tell me until much later one week we were at the Salvation Army store he said I hid them between his books on the corridor, Silvia says, another week we were on our way to the child psychologist he said I hid them behind the bookshelf in his kitchen, Silvia says, in the cabinet by the sink, places in that apartment I continue to imagine after all these years for no reason the other day I was listening to an interview with Glenn Gould who was answering a question about whether he listens to his piano recordings from years ago, Silvia says, my father wrote about Glenn Gould and his vacuum cleaner, Eva says, Esteban would say to me whenever you're vacuuming Roberto Carlos is probably imagining cataclysmic sandstorms please don't vacuum near Roberto Carlos, Silvia says, I like the image of your son imagining what Roberto Carlos's imagining, Eva says, Esteban said his earliest memory is from when his sister was born because it was the first time he'd been away from me he had to stay with his father while I was in the hospital his father had tried to calm him by offering ice cream he accepted the ice cream of course but doesn't remember having the ice cream just the feeling of being away from me which doesn't make any sense because when Juliet was born he was eight years old, Silvia says, sometimes for no reason I imagine the social worker's dorm room in Santa Cruz the dorm room isn't a slab of concrete but an open house by the sea, Silvia says, I still remember a balcony by the sea in Santa Cruz where a physics major tried to woo me by explaining the plot of The Loser by Thomas Bernhard, Eva says, better The Loser than his poems on the humorous trajectories of neutrons, Silvia says, Glenn Gould as Sir John by the bridge of the Hudson River, Silvia thinks, before Glenn Gould answered the question of whether he listened to his recordings from years ago he pretended to be a stuffy English actor called Sir John who's bashful about whether he watches himself in his old films can I play it for you, Silvia says, who doesn't love Glenn doing voices, Eva says, Silvina Ocampo search for Glenn Gould interview + Sir John, Silvia says, that was the film we did in America wasn't it, Glenn Gould says [in an exaggerated English accent], back in the '50s, very awkward location, fairly contaminated streams, marshy, mosquitoes even, no sense of landscape architecture the Americans [Silvia & Eva laugh], after my father died I reread his novels, Eva says, searching for clues for unspecified riddles, Silvia says, he mentions Glenn Gould & the vacuum in passing in one of his novels but doesn't explain the joke I had to searched it online sometimes on our way to City Lights Books my father would tell me about his research on Freud & Ferenczi & Parapsychology, for instance, Eva says, I don't know about Freud or Fifirinczi but I know about Ouija boards and telepathy, Silvia says, Ferenczi writes to Freud saying palm reading isn't that different than this psychotherapy business you're trying to kickstart and Freud replies don't go there mine has to become a respectable business, Eva says, do you want me to read your palm I enrolled in an online palm reading course once, Silvia says, Eva is scanning Silvia, Eva says [Eva & Silvia laugh], this is what is called the Line Line, Silvia says, the Line that tickles, Eva says, a linear Line Line means you will dream of highways, Silvia says, tonight I will dream of Roberto Carlos in a sandstorm, Eva says, my mother used to sing that one famous Roberto Carlos song to Esteban at bedtime, Silvia says, tu eres mi hermano del alma realmente el amigo, Eva sings, que en todo camino y jornada esta siempre conmigo, Silvia sings, Freud calls the phenomenon thought transference whereas for Ferenczi when two people sit and talk they turn into mediums for each other, Eva says, transference from patients to rats will present unprecedented difficulties, Silvia says, so instead of saying to you be my friend I should say be my psychic, Eva says, can we take a break and start again tomorrow how long are you staying in Buenos Aires let me show you where the ghost of Martha Argerich hangs out, Silvia says, does the ghost of Martha Argerich also cancels her appearances at the last minute or, Eva says, sshh, Silvia says, she can hear us.

Aura's Mother

I am not Jacques Austerlitz, Aura says, my mind, unbeknownst to me, has not been drawing me toward train stations that are linked to an unpleasant past I have forgotten, nor has my mind been protecting me from my unpleasant past, and unlike Jacques Austerlitz's Welsh parents my American parents were unfortunately not cold and distant but super nice can you please delete the word super from the transcript I don't want to sound superduper, Aura says, all supers will be expunged from the record, Ada says, I am not anyone's victim, Aura says, you're a professor of Latin American literature, Ada says, I was, yes, Aura says, until they banned Latin American literature from the curriculum, Ada says, even if the Americans kill me and I return as a ghost my haunting wouldn't be hey why did you kill me but I have come to tell you I am not your victim, Aura says, I am not your victim even if you killed me, Aura says, or I am but I refuse to play the role of the victim because that's what the placid American killers want, Aura says, that's what they've always wanted, Ada says, look at the poor suffering Latinas and so on, Aura says, and yet here we are about to talk about how the Americans abducted me as a child, Aura says, we can always skip the topic and talk about Doctor Sueño's latest transmission if you, Ada says, my super American father would attend my soccer games and my super American mother would bake me banana bread for breakfast, Aura says, close parenthesis and say that's all folks!, Aura says, my super American father would pay me five dollars a goal when I was little and ten per goal when the field tripled in size and my output of goals dwindled, Aura says, I still remember my father on the sidelines shouting move up / move up during my soccer matches, Ada says, move up as in he wanted you to play as a forward even if you were a defender or, Aura says, all soccer fathers want their soccer daughters to be a center forward, Ada says, when my mother was dying I thought she was going to reveal some great truth about my adoption like in those maudlin narratives whereas on her deathbed the mom feels transcendental regret and so on, Aura says, I prefer absurd deathbed scenes like Senges's reinterpretation of Goethe's last words but that's neither here nor, Ada says, but my mother died content about her happy life and so did my father, Aura says, your parents never told you you were adopted, Ada says, of course they did but not until I asked them, Aura says, they wanted to perform the You are Our Real Daughter Even If We Are Not Your Real Parents skit, and even though I knew they were performing this skit due to a dearth of imagination and a desire to think of themselves as humans abloom in love and so on, I didn't want to disappoint them by calling them out on it and saying quit it with your pantomime of parental love, although I know a pantomime of parental love isn't any different from what we like to call parental love, so when I was in high school I asked my super American parents if I was adopted and they brewed green Jasmine tea and garlanded themselves with comfortable Sunday clothes and said yes dear and performed their skit of Adopted Love and that was that, you didn't talk about it again, Ada says, I was already sick of their green tea by then, Aura says, and one day my parents died and the topic died with them, Aura says, until one day, Ada says, why are you in such a hurry to get to the until one day part, Aura says, I'm sorry I thought you, Ada says, you thought Aura must be eager to tell her story, which she needs in order to live, Aura says, my father hated that cliché about humans needing stories in order to live, Ada says, I read that your father thought of himself as an anti-novelist because the role of the anti-christ was already taken, Aura says, when I was twelve he bought me an enormous bookcase and every week I would look forward to going to the bookstore with him so I could fill up my enormous bookcase, Ada says, so given that you probably read most of the books in that enormous bookcase plus other books in other enormous bookcases you probably already know what happens in the until one day part of my story, Aura says, more or less, Ada says, go on then, Aura says, I would be embarrassed to, Ada says, blah blah go on, Aura says, until one day Aura went through her parents' belongings, Ada says, which Aura was planning to discard, Aura says, and she found an adoption document that included the name of her former parents, Ada says, the name of her foster home not of her former parents, Aura says, years went by and one day, Ada says, when my mother died I didn't grieve so I thought well that's because my father is still alive, Aura says, but when my father died and I still didn't grieve I wondered what these human attachments meant to me, and whether we invent these attachments to make us feel more like the characters in the maudlin narratives we like about ourselves, and later I tried on the narrative of oh I didn't grieve for them because they weren't my real parents but that wasn't it either, plus you knew this real parents explanation was another one of those narrative clichés, Ada says, one day they were there, Aura says, performing their parental skits, one day they weren't there anymore, you didn't miss them, Ada says, I missed them on Sundays because that's when I would visit them but I play ping pong on Sundays now so soon I won't miss them anymore, Aura says, by the way I know that while we've been talking you probably have been wondering how to ask me more questions that will disinter more details about my life, Aura says, details that will particularize my abduction story since all American abductions stories are alike but don't you think these details, these costume changes, this mania for the gadgetry of, Aura says, we can invoke magicians or John Cage and pull details out of a hat if you would rather, Ada says, we need a Pale American nurse that comes into the hospital room in Jacksonville where my mother is dying and says to me only family members are allowed, followed by an earnest meditation on race, Aura says, my father was always pointing out narrative clichés for my sister and I during dinner he hated those American novels that begin with the usual trauma / banal combo, for instance, Ada says, give me an example, Aura says, on the day my father was dying I received a brand new edition of How To Make Friends and Influence People, Ada says, on the day I was abducted the weather was super nice, Aura says, on the day my father was captured by the American abductors I received a love letter from Carlitos, Ada says, poor Carlitos forever sending love letters at the wrong time, Aura says, reader I married Carlitos, Ada says, on the day I read an expose about how my foster home was shut down because of its tenebrous links to the American abductions of Latin American children at the border the birds were singing, Aura says, reader I lied I didn't marry Carlitos Carlitos was deported a long time ago, Ada says, I didn't lie about the birds singing although maybe they were not singing but consorting about who to peck to death next, Aura says, and I will not lie about how the news of my tenebrous foster home affected my imagination.

Silvia's Son

Whatever happened to Roberto Carlos, Eva thinks as she falls asleep, The Loser equals Glenn greater than everyone except Martha, Silvia thinks as she falls asleep, are you sleeping already or, Juliet says, the show will go on despite the sandstorm, Roberto Carlos says, thanks to me Glenn plays the piano like a typewriter, the vacuum says, I remember the first time I listened to the walls, Silvina Ocampo says, it was a marshy day, mosquitoes even, you know storytelling isn't allowed here, Silvina, the Censor says, wall / ear on wall / raccoons / ear infection / otoscope / earwax mines is that better, Silvina Ocampo says, what does the wall say, Raccoona Sheldon says, for years I've been finding coloring pencils in my oatmeal, the physics professor says, my father would take me to the Botanical Gardens every morning and perform magic tricks for me, Martha Argerich says, she doesn't know where her son is, Eva thinks as she awakes, where are you going so early do you have a breakfast date you forgot to tell me your dreams, Juliet says, when I was pregnant with Esteban my playing slowed down, Silvia says, I wasn't as tempestuous as I preferred although no one seemed to notice except me I would say to Esteban in the Womb did you nip a millisecond out of my tempo, do you remember what you would play for Esteban in the Womb, Eva says, Ondine, Silvia says, I would imagine Esteban as a water nymph which is not a very practical occupation I know, Silvia says, Esteban saying I see your toes on the pedals, mom, Silvia thinks, Esteban once wrote in one of those sentimental essays schoolchildren are asked to write on mother's day that he remembered my toes the most, Silvia says, she no longer cares if her son hates her, Eva thinks, although of course she does, I used to hide under the piano and watch your toes on the pedals Esteban told me when he was a senior in high school, weeks before he graduated and ran away from me, Silvia says, that was the last time you saw your son, Eva says, when he was five years old I was invited to perform a small piano tour in Panama I remember Esteban and I sitting in the back of this long shark car for hours as we were driven from town to town sometimes I wonder if this is one of those series of moments that add up to him hating me thank you for not saying I am sure he doesn't hate you, Silvia says, my father would make candy appear on my head, Martha Argerich says, how do you say Chiriquí, Esteban would say, Silvia thinks, after one of these small town concerts people gathered around me to ask for my autograph later Esteban said he was alarmed at these people crowding around me so he bit one of them, Silvia says, I don't understand I'm sorry how is the shark car one of the moments that adds up to, Eva says, you forgot to ask me what did I play in my small town piano tour, Silvia says, Ondine, Eva says, Gaspard de la Nuit, yes, Silvia says, did Esteban in the Womb who was no longer in the womb remember Ondine of course not that's a dumb question I'm sorry, Eva says, my father preserved my appendix in a jar, Martha Argerich says, Esteban would hide under the piano when I was practicing so he heard Ondine in my womb, in the piano's womb as an audience in Chiriquí, as a tune he would murmur in the back of the shark car, Silvia says, tonight I will dream of your son murmuring Ondine, Eva thinks, when we were crossing the desert one of the American abductors who looked as if he could move a grand piano on his back captured us shackled us in the back of his patrol car Esteban and I remained just as silent as we'd been in the back of the shark car the American abductor asked Esteban if he believed in UFOs no sir Esteban said, I've seen their flashing lights I've seen them hovering over this side of the desert on nights like this, he said, have you heard of our new tracking program, he said, no I said, we're piloting a program with the governments of El Salvador and Honduras and Guatemala to implant a tracker on you people who have a high probability of attempting to cross our border, he said, what's an implant, mother, Esteban said, we shoot you with our implant gun and the tracking device lives inside your skin, he said, we come at night and shoot you with our implants so the question is did I find you because of your implants or because of our surveillance satellites orbiting the earth, he said, we don't have implants, I said to Esteban, not yet, he said, he's just trying to scare us, I said, I haven't even began to try to scare you, he said, I've never heard of that program, Eva says, assume the back of the shark car is a warm memory of childhood for Esteban, Silvia says, now assume the back of the patrol car is a terrifying memory of childhood for Esteban, Silvia says, both reasonable assumptions, Eva says, assume time doesn't exist in Esteban's memory or in his dreams or while he's coughing out his appendix or in his journals if he keeps any how would I know if the back of those cars is happening at the same time for him but let's assume, Silvia says, Esteban murmurs

Ondine while imagining a tracking device inside his skin, Eva says, his hands feeling both the wind outside the window in Panama and the handcuffs on his lap in Texas, Silvia says, seeing the palm trees of Chiriquí and the dark desert of Texas at the same time, Eva says, if I would have given him one or the other I think he could have forgiven me, Silvia says, but I am responsible for both, Silvia says, both were too much for him, Silvia thinks, not just both but everything else he had to endure, Silvia says, the American detention centers for Latin Americans which I will not describe for you even if you ask me, Silvia says, search for them online if you want, Silvia says, they overcrowded us in a room with no ventilation someone screamed a scorpion / a scorpion everyone panicked but we couldn't get out, Silvia thinks, the child psychologist said Esteban told him he often dreamed of faceless people banging their heads on windows, Silvia says, thank you for not pointing out that my theory on the juxtaposition of seemingly related moments in the back of two cars as the source of my son's hate is ridiculous, Silvia says, thank you for not saying no Silvia that's not ridiculous, Silvia says, when he turned eleven I bought him a birdcage and a caique, Silvia says, tonight I will dream of your son with a birdcage on his lap in the back of the shark car, Eva thinks, I said happy birthday my love, Silvia says, caique parrots are beloved for their playful curiosity and silly antics, I said, quoting an online article on the three ways to know if a caique parrot is right for you, what were the three ways, Eva says, assess your lifestyle, decide if you can live with nipping, figure out how much time you have for a caique, Silvia says, I said what are you going to call your caique, Silvia says, I said I think we can live with nipping don't you think, Silvia says, but Esteban didn't say anything.

Aura's Mother

I don't remember my abduction, Aura says, you were four years old, Ada says, I don't remember my former parents or the particulars of the foster home, Aura says, what's your earliest memory of childhood, Ada says, I haven't imagined what my former parents were like but I have imagined the day my latter parents arrived to the foster home where I was detained, Aura says, although before I imagined them I imagined me driving to the shuttered foster home and entering through a cracked window into an office space empty of foster things but full of my outsized contemplation in what's known as my Arvo Pärt contemplative moment, Aura says, the Samuel Barber Adagio for Strings moment, Ada says, the Gorecki's Symphony No. 3 moment, Aura says, do you mind if we listen to the Adagio for Strings, Aura says, I would rather listen to a parody of it but if you, Ada says, don't switch off your recorder though, Aura says, Leonora stream Adagio for String by Samuel Barber, Ada says, he disappeared into the shadows with a little bird's laugh, which I did not like, Leonora Carrington says, don't mind her she's set to random, Ada says, is she set to pick a specific version of the Adagio or,

Aura says, since I'm her main source of data inputs probably a fast version with wrong notes, Ada says, adagio prestissimo for strings, with upsies, the word upsies also to be expunged, obviously, Aura says, can Leonora connect to your sound system, Ada says, as long as she doesn't stop recording us, Aura says, are you awake, Eva says, transcribing a recording of someone I interviewed today, yes, Ada says, same, Eva says, who did you, Ada says, I can't tell you her name but I can tell you Roberto Carlos was the name of her son's pet rat, Eva says, the professor I interviewed today told me she used to have a hamster called Hamster, Ada says, oh can I hear about Hamster it's late here in Buenos Aires and I, Eva says, I can't sleep either, Ada says, Leonora stream Aura & Hamster, Ada says, a bell rang for dinner, Leonora Carrington says, soon after my father brought me my first hamster, Aura says, when I was still in first grade, I think, my cousin came to visit and said why isn't your hamster moving, so I prodded Hamster with a puzzle piece, do you remember what kind of puzzle, Ada says, I can't believe you asked her what kind of puzzle, Eva says, and since Hamster didn't move I said Hamster is sleeping, Aura says, and later I told my dad look Hamster has been sleeping for a while, and the next day Hamster wasn't there and I said where is Hamster and dad said Hamster was sick so I took him to the hospital, and six years later he brought me an identical hamster and said at last Hamster is back from the hospital, but of course by then I knew Hamster had been dead all along so that became our joke every time a new Hamster died, how many Hamsters did your father bring you, Ada says, like ten, Aura says, and later, after I traded my parents for college, my dad started breeding hamsters at home, that's beautiful but a bit too symbolic for my, Eva says, I know I didn't transcribe this part, Ada says, but perhaps we need these outward symbolic activities so our imagination can continue to output new scenarios in which our loved ones are still with us, Ada says, like you and I and these interviews Tata couldn't complete, Eva says, I've started imagining that Tata brought me a hamster called Hamster when I was little isn't that silly, Ada says, is that the Adagio for Strings in the background are you okay, Eva says, sleep let's talk tomorrow, Ada says, at last Roberto Carlos is back from the hospital, Ada, Ada's father says, all rodents will be expunged from the record, Eva, Sir John says, Mehr Licht, Goethe says, could we spend recess together I could tell you my dreams from last night, Carlitos says, the joke being that Mehr Licht doesn't equate to more light but more Lichtenberg, Glenn Gould says, I have come from the future to tell you if my Anywhere Door doesn't work you can borrow my Sequence Spray, Aura, Doraemon says, my American parents arrive to the foster home early in the morning because they paid extra to have first picks, Aura says, I don't know if that's how American adoptions work but if you, Ada says, and because the night before they consulted their friends about which clothes would be interpreted by the children & staff as most optimal for the benign rearing of children, they are wearing their optimized clothes you can interject and add to it, Ada, otherwise you're just recording my same old invented version, Aura says, the mother had been against asking their friends about which clothes to wear because they didn't have real friends and she didn't like talking to their imaginary friends as much as her husband did, Ada says, the father had been against bringing their imaginary friends to the foster home but there they were, Aura says, we will leave it up to our listeners to imagine what their imaginary friends were wearing, Ada says, I am four years old but I already know that the more forlorn I look the less likely I am to be chosen by the optimized Pale Americans, Aura says, but the four year old didn't yet know that most optimized Pale Americans are taught in school that Pale Americans are born to be world saviors, Ada says, so the more forlorn she looked the more likely she was to be chosen, Aura says, can we talk about something else, Aura says, anything you, Ada says, do you know how old Jacques Austerlitz was when he suddenly remembered what happened to him as a child, Aura says, halfway through the novel I think Leonora search for, Ada says, Austerlitz says he's four and a half years old when he arrives to England from Germany in 1939, Aura says, and he tells the narrator about suddenly remembering what happened to him as a child in 1996 so that means he's approximately sixty one and a half years old when he remembers meeting his Welsh parents who weren't his real parents at the Liverpool Street Station, and so sometimes I think when I am sixty one and a half years old I will suddenly remember my former mother, Aura says, no Adagio for Strings please, Aura says, the memory of himself as a four year old comes to him because Austerlitz can't sleep so he exhausts himself by walking around London so perhaps you could accelerate the process of remembering by, Ada says, let's talk about something else, Aura says, I can recommend the best green tea in town, Aura says, or we can conjecture about why we haven't been deported yet, Aura says, or I can tell you about the DNA tests I underwent last week to find my former parents.

Silvia's Son

What I remember the most is the temporary houses in San Bruno and San Francisco and Oakland, Silvia says, what I remember the most, Silvia says, I like how saying what I remember the most contributes to the illusion of a finality to the apparatus of remembrance, Silvia says, why are you so quiet today, Silvia says, the psychic life takes its toll doesn't it, Silvia says, I'm sorry I wasn't going to tell you but I'm too embarrassed to go on without telling you I dreamed of Esteban last night, Eva says, was he hiding his coloring pencils in a waiting room for fax machines, Silvia says, I can't remember the dream but when I awoke I knew I had dreamed of him all night, Eva says, where are you in this dream you can't remember, Silvia says, I'm on a bench next to him we're tourists we're waiting for a café to open, Eva says, what does Esteban say in this dream you can't remember, Silvia says, this café is known for its carrot walnut muffins, Eva says, what does the dream mean, Silvia says, that I want to be you, Eva thinks, that I wish there was a door on your back that I could open so I could be there with you instead of over here across this table, Eva says, I would prefer an Anywhere

Door on my back but thank you, Silvia says, The Lady with an Anywhere Door on her Back by Dr. Seuss, Eva says, Silvia is scanning Eva, Silvia says, before my father would tell us an anecdote he would say do you want to hear it dramatically, melodramatically, or obliquely, Eva says, do you sometimes remember your father in those three modalities at the same time or, Silvia says, my father never told me about his time in the American detention camp system for Latin Americans in any modality and never wrote about it either, Eva says, when misfortune befalls you you're embarrassed to share it because you know others will think it was probably your fault, Silvia says, he used to tell me he didn't write about it because others had it worse than him and there was plenty of footage of the American detention camps for Latin Americans and plenty of documentaries about the abuses there but you're right he was probably embarrassed, Eva says, my father the sophisticated writer with the mid level office job crammed in a tent in the desert, Eva says, the sophisticated writer, Silvia says, that was a joke from when we used to live together in San Francisco, Eva says, what was the joke if you don't mind, Silvia says, I'm a sophisticated writer I can't do the dishes today, my father would say, Eva says, I can't take out the garbage I can't speak to other adults especially parents oh please not the parents he rarely spoke to anyone except us my sister imitated him at this not speaking to others outside the household, what do you remember the most about that time, Silvia says, this is a trick question isn't it, Eva says, I wish my apparatus of remembrance allowed me to remember what I said earlier about people saying what I remember the most we need to review the transcript from a minute ago, Silvia says, I remember one summer a writer from Quito came to visit my father and they talked and talked in our kitchen in

San Francisco and afterward my mother said I miss hearing you laugh, Tato, Eva says, he didn't consort with American writers, Silvia says, I didn't know about it then but when he'd already been deported to Bogotá he wrote in Spanish about the mindboggling racism of so-called Progressive American writers, Eva says, do you know if he was detained at Fort Sill, Silvia says, I sued to obtain his deportation records his forms did include the location of the camps where he'd been detained while waiting to be deported let me check the names Taryn Simon retrieve records of my father's deportation, Eva says, this is probably from before the news reports about private prison companies lengthening the deportation process to maximize their profits, Silvia says, before Latin Americans weren't allowed to leave the country unless they surrendered themselves to these private assembly lines of deportations, yes, Eva says, McAllen in Texas, Berks in Pennsylvania, here, Fort Sill, Eva says, do you want to hear about my time in Fort Sill dramatically, melodramatically, or obliquely, Silvia says, obliquely but if you don't feel like, Eva says, due to circumstances I have mostly not forgotten my son ran away from me, Silvia says, this would be a good time for that door to materialize on your back, Eva says, at night the American abductors would barge into the room where Esteban and I were sleeping they would demand that I sign our deportation papers at first I would try to reason with them if we go back to Guatemala the police will kill us like they killed my parents we don't believe you they would say so I stopped trying to reason with them I am not signing anything we could barely sleep waiting for them to barge in two or three times a week what afflicted us wasn't insomnia it was something else like a constant state of hypnagogia like in your art installation, Silvia says, you searched my name before meeting with me, Eva says, I was inside your installation in Santiago de Chile years ago I didn't know it was your installation until I searched you again last night, Silvia says, hyperventilate yourself and transport whatever you hallucinate to the next module, Taryn Simon says, your watch interjects at random like that or, Silvia says, merge your hallucination with the first creature that comes to mind and carry it to the next module, Taryn Simon says, I programmed Taryn Simon to interject relevantly the word hypnagogia is rarely used so that word must have been the trigger, Eva says, when I was inside Hypnagogia I thought I wish I could come here every day to mourn, Silvia says, that's the nicest thing anyone, Eva says, I didn't even need a door when I hyperventilated per your instructions I transported my Esteban saying why can't you get me out of here, Silvia says, I transported the American abductors waking Esteban and I in the middle of the night, Silvia says, the American abductors saying follow us you have a dental appointment ask me how many of them, Silvia says, how many of them, Eva says, I didn't count them seven or eight of them three of them were filming us with their devices while narrating the proceedings we are escorting two filthy animals to the parking lot outside wait we can't have the three of you narrating they stopped us while they did rock paper scissors we are at a crucial juncture in our proceeding whoever wins will become the narrator Esteban didn't even look up in the parking lot outside they gathered around a school bus they opened the rear door one of them said put your son there we're shipping him to a foster home we are at a crucial juncture in our proceeding when the mother has to let go of her son so he can be adopted by a more civilized family everyone was laughing at the mocking voice of the narrator until my son started screaming, Silvia says, no, he screamed, Silvia says, don't let them take me, he screamed, I thought he was going to faint from screaming so much I saw how the faces of the American abductors went dark they were used to us crying and pleading and screaming but not like Esteban was screaming for years I've imagined the seven or eight of them dreaming of a faraway tower where they think they're safe at last but then my son's screams approach them like a wind and their faces go dark again, Silvia says, I'm sorry I couldn't merge my hallucination with the first creature that came to mind do you need a moment, Silvia says, yes thank you, Eva says, here I'll take over, Silvia says, and so Eva asked Silvia if the American abductors took her son away from her, Silvia says, and Silvia said not that time, Eva, not that time, and Eva and Silvia opened their Anywhere Door and they were gone.

Aura's Mother

I didn't want to be the child who sets out on a journey to find her former parents, Aura says, or traces of her former parents, and when I say a child I mean me, obviously, a thirty year old former professor, in other words I always skip the second half of Austerlitz when Jacques sets on a journey to Prague to learn about his parents, Aura says, but, Ada says, what if we forego this narrative but conjunction for a bit what would we talk about, Aura says, do you ever dream of Jacques Austerlitz's Liverpool Street Station, Ada says, once I dreamed I had a daughter who drew one of the fortresses from Austerlitz, Aura says, where are you in the dream, Ada says, I am reading in the kitchen table next to my daughter, Aura says, what does your daughter say, Ada says, look at my star shaped building like in the picture, Aura says, what do you think the dream means, Ada says, it's unfair to my latter parents this search for my former parents and it's ridiculous for me to slot myself into this In Search of Aura's Former Parents, Aura says, in today's episode of In Search Of our protagonist spouts clichés like it's unfair for my latter parents this search for me former parents, Aura says, in tomorrow's episode a nursebot will extract Aura's DNA while sipping from her green tea, Aura says, in the day after tomorrow's episode Dr. Zodiac Pérez will smuggle Aura's DNA out of the United States and into Argentina because Latin Americans in the United States are banned from this type of DNA matching why aren't you interfering with my episodes, Aura says, I'm sorry I was still at the Liverpool Street Station, Ada says, where are you in the station, Aura says, I don't know if I should, Ada says, out with it or no more episodes of The Weekly Aches of Aura Smith, Aura says, I am not in the station you are, Ada says, according to my foster documents I was four and a half years old when I entered the foster office space for abducted children, Aura says, the same age as Jacques Austerlitz when he arrives at the Liverpool Street Station in 1939, where, according to my imagination, you are a girl waiting on a bench, Ada says, a girl who's wearing a white dress Alice in Wonderland might have worn to her first communion, last night I reread that passage where Jacques, at sixty one and half years old, remembers himself at four and a half years old at the Liverpool Street Station for the first time, Aura says, is it strange that I reread that passage too probably not that strange since yesterday you said you were not Jacques Austerlitz, Ada says, and I not only saw the minister and his wife, said Austerlitz, Leonora Carrington reads, I also saw the boy they had come to meet, Aura says, he was sitting by himself on a bench over to one side, Leonora Carrington reads, his legs, in white knee length socks, did not reach the floor, Aura says, and for the small rucksack he was holding on his lap I don't think I would have known him, Austerlitz said, what if the episodes of In Search Of were told from the point of view of my DNA, Aura says, I know you know that's a terrible idea, Aura, Aura says,

Jacques recognizes the boy as himself because of the rucksack, Aura says, which comes up before but without any linkage to 1939, Ada says, there's even a photograph of the rucksack, yes, Aura says, so of course I've wondered what if when I am sixty one and a half I suddenly remember myself at four and a half but can't recognize myself as myself due to a lack of rucksack, Aura says, and even if I do recognize myself no algorithm will be able to match the image of my former mother in my head with an image of my former mother in storage somewhere, Aura says, your mother when you were four and a half years old, Ada says, moreover the moment I will at last remember her will also be the moment I will begin to erode her since every retrieval erodes the memory of that which we've retrieved, Aura says, when will you know if your DNA, Ada says, any minute now a heybot from the Banco Nacional de Datos Genéticos will message me and inform me that after applying the latest technologies, Aura says, which have automated the matching of DNAs, unlike back in the day when the matching between the grandmothers and the children who were abducted by the Argentinian military was more manual ask me why the grandmothers not the parents, Aura says, because the parents of the abducted children were murdered by the Argentinian military, Ada says, my parents were probably deported, Aura says, who knows to where I don't want to be the child who says I know in my heart they are still alive and imagines her heart like one of those metal detectors at the beach, do you ever dream of this DNA matching procedure, Ada says, we're already in the but part of my But I did become the child who sets out on a journey to find her former parents, Ada, Aura says, but yes, I have imagined the matching procedure as a (1) sorrowful old man from Fritz Lang's Nibelungen film opening door after door inside a tower and saying sorry to interrupt is my mother here by any chance, (2) Jerry Lewis trying to fit my DNA part with every DNA part passing through an assembly line, (3) a vast field populated with mountains of garbage and Wall-E sifting through it all to find me a match, (4) a bird that's also a dog following her nose to wherever mom and dad are did you know that some of the abducted children in Argentina waited for their military parents to die before going to the Banco Nacional de Datos Genéticos to avoid upsetting their military parents, Aura says, to avoid them being imprisoned as a result of a potential DNA match, yes, Ada says, so of course I've wondered if my mind had been secretly waiting for my American parents to die so that I can begin my In Search Of, Aura says, someone is throwing rocks at your window or, Ada says, those are bugs killing themselves because of the heat, Aura says, which they weren't expecting in this part of the United States did you notice that before Jacques remembers himself at four and a half he associates the Liverpool Street Station with a seventeenth century insane asylum, Aura says, plus graveyards, Ada says, a bit overwrought though you don't notice it until the twelfth time you read it, Aura says, right because he's been talking about architecture for like 135 pages prior to arriving to the Liverpool Street Station so you think the seventeenth century insane asylum, which was built either on or near the Liverpool Street Station, and the multiple layers of graveyards underneath London, are more of the same architectural musings, Ada says, these dark associations work because like Austerlitz the reader doesn't yet know that in 1939 his former parents, fearing for his life, arranged for his escape from Prague on a train to England, Aura says, Jacques sits at his train station and tries to imagine where the inmates of the insane asylum used to be confined, Ada says, and whether their accumulated suffering has ebbed away or it can still be sensed like the cold wind on his face now that's overwrought, Aura says, I'll skip my overwrought question for now then, Ada says, in which Aura encourages Ada to share her overwrought question, Aura says, what do you think you will imagine at the equivalent of your train station, Ada says, not people confined in an insane asylum, Aura says, not myself in a white straitjacket in a white padded room without windows, Aura says, not my already old former parents arriving at the station at last and embracing me, Aura says, not Doraemon lending me his Sequence Spray and me spraying it on a photo of me at my train station so I can find out what happens next, Aura says, how did you and Doraemon, Ada says, my father was an executive at a transnational bank and he wanted to learn more about the possibilities of AI for his business unit so during a summer vacation in London he took us to an exhibit at the Barbican called AI More Than Human, which included Doraemon as an early example of robots in pop culture, Aura says, after we were done with the exhibit he bought me a Doraemon boxset, Aura says, ask me why I haven't gone back to my own version of Jacques' train station, also known as the Adelanto Foster Home, Aura says, because you don't want to hallucinate like Jacques does while at the train station, Ada says, it's been demolished, Aura says, but if you're a member you can enter Ambient Cannabis, the new white box of a store that has been built there, Aura says, there's one around the corner from here, Ada says, I don't think Alice in Wonderland would show up to her first communion, Aura says, oh that was yes you're probably right, Ada says, we could wait at the Ambient Cannabis around the corner for the heybots to reach me they have different mood rooms there, Aura says, the Bliss Room, Aura says, the Sleep Room, Ada says, the Relief Room, Aura says, unless you already exhausted all your questions?

Part VI

Roberto's Father

Neuronal substrate of the cognitive map, Roberto Bolaño reads, nickname for your new sidekick or, Ulises Lima says, automatic stimulations of the medial forebrain bundle, Roberto Bolaño reads, that's a bit long for a nickname but to quote the manuals of excessive mirth I appreciate the enthusiasm, Ulises Lima says, where's your grandfather, Roberto Bolaño says, my grandfather had Alzheimer's, Ulises Lima says, and when the American abductors captured him they placed him in solitary confinement for weeks, you want to tell him you're sorry and so on, Roberto Bolaño says, my grandfather doesn't show up in my dreams and the dream exercises aren't helping, Ulises Lima says, mice were implanted with polytrodes in the CA1 pyramidal layer and stimulation electrodes in the medial forebrain bundle, Roberto Bolaño reads, is that from our virtual library do we even have a virtual library, Ulises Lima says, I appreciate the enthusiasm isn't a direct quote from any manual of anything, Roberto Bolaño says, one day my grandfather could no longer tell what an oven was for, one day he was punished for what he could no longer tell, Ulises Lima says, close your eyes and repeat after me, Roberto Bolaño says, close your eyes and repeat after me, Ulises Lima says, I am in solitary confinement, Roberto Bolaño says, I am in solitary confinement, Ulises Lima says, I see signals from electrodes being transmitted into a unity gain headstage preamplifier I haven't spoken with anyone in weeks I am thirsty, Roberto Bolaño says, I can't do this, Ulises Lima says, sponge from the specialists, Roberto Bolaño says, ready, set, the pause is implied my name is Roberto Bolaño Gonzalez I am in solitary confinement I haven't seen my son in weeks and for reasons I don't want to get into I am tying a bedsheet around my neck and hanging myself, I'm sorry, Ulises Lima says, guilt is boring and so are the readymades of grief, Roberto Bolaño says, in this study we used the spontaneous activity of a given place cell during sleep to trigger automatically rewarding stimulations of the medial forebrain bundle (MFB) to create an artificial place / reward association, Roberto Bolaño reads, I am not repeating that after you, Ulises Lima says, I wrote a letter to the doctor of this article dear Dr. Benchenane I hope you aren't dead I read your 2015 study about implanting pleasant associations into the memories of mice I read you are ready to experiment with humans I hereby would like to confirm that I am human and therefore qualify for your upcoming experiments, Roberto Bolaño reads, what's the experiment is he going to implant mice on your brain ask him if the price of shaving your head is included, Ulises Lima says, prolong your sleepless hours by activating the chit / chat setting on your robots this human needs to pretend to sleep for a few hours, Roberto Bolaño says, I need an interlude too, Robert Desnos says, I'm going to say a word and you will tell me what comes to mind, Doctor Sueño says, clouds, Robert Desnos says, permanent press, Roberto

Bolaño says, I have come to tell you it wasn't a misunderstanding, the loudspeaker says, you will never retrieve someone like me, the egg sandwich says, that's so rude go to your room, the chicken sandwich says, why are your eyeballs still open, Rob Ott says, you can't open eyeballs unless you slice them like in that Buñuel film, Wall-E, Roberto Bolaño says, I have computed your response as a diversion whose objective is to confuse my subsequent output, Rob Ott says, primary.objective.unmet., Roberto Bolaño says, I have computed your response as mockery of prehistoric robot speak, Rob Ott says, which A has no impact on me because I have never spoken like that and B because I wasn't programmed to have feelings ha pause for effect ha, have you been eavesdropping on me am I even awake, Roberto Bolaño says, I have been programmed to record everything within a radius whose length I cannot disclose as to whether you are awake I would be happy to pinch you if pincers are provided, Rob Ott says, so if you have been inputting our voices you can output imitations of our voices, Roberto Bolaño says, you are correct, correct underlined, Rob Ott says, replicate me, C-3PO, Roberto Bolaño says, I am maybe Roberto Bolaño I am afraid of my story correction I am not afraid of my story what were they and so on every day my father is still dead, Rob Ott says, I know Ulises Lima sent you as payback for asking him to let me sleep, Roberto Bolaño says, that is not possible due to Ulises Lima is a character from a novel ha pause for affect ha, Rob Ott says, roll on to your charging station and let me at least attempt to asleep, Mazinger, Roberto Bolaño says, your.wish.has.been.granted did you see what I did there double ha plus pause, Rob Ott says, neuronal substrate of the cognitive map, Roberto Bolaño thinks, medial forebrain bundle, the keyword says, tres tristes tigres comen trigo en el trigal, Antonio's daughter says, if you are having the same dream during your REM cycle that simplifies our task, Dr. Zodiac Perez says, because we can pair your REM with the positive stimulation electrodes in your MFB, transference from patient to mice will present unprecedented difficulties, Dr. Benchenane says, I sleep on my feet, Robert Desnos says, which isn't the same as sleepwalking, did you bring me a drill this time, Roberto Bolaño says, not this time but I can share my mortadella sandwich with you, Antonio says, good morning our Roberto didn't sleep well last night please be gentle with him, Ulises Lima says, they plant cauliflowers and groundhogs in the garden here, Roberto Bolaño says, why does he always interject is he worried you're going to report him or, Antonio says, ask him about his grandfather, Roberto Bolaño says, tell me about your grandfather, Antonio says, my grandfather's name was Noel and he would let me paint rainbows on his face while he snored on the couch, Ulises Lima says, how old were you, Antonio says, my grandfather was seventy two and I was ten and when the American abductors captured him they placed him in solitary confinement, Ulises Lima says, he died not knowing where he was, Roberto Bolaño says, how do you know this, Antonio says, neither one of us can sleep so late at night we perform the Didi & Nurse Show, Roberto Bolaño says, my grandfather built a house for the migrants who would pass through the fields of his farm in El Salvador, Ulises Lima says, and even though he didn't have that much money whenever he could he would bring them fruit, his grandfather would dream of the wind sending down its spies upon that house again, Roberto Bolaño says, where is that from, Antonio says, tell him about your rat experiment, Ulises Lima says, if you read the wind sent down its spies upon the house again you still have to imagine the wind and the spies and the house and the previous times the wind sent its spies upon the house again, Roberto Bolaño says, tell me about your rat experiment, Antonio says, your daughter's dream what does it mean, Roberto Bolaño says, which dream the one about speaking all the languages in the world, Antonio says, Eva can speak all the languages in the world, Roberto Bolaño reads, and when she speaks Spanish to her Spanish teacher her words come out as blah blah blah, although her Spanish teacher understands what Eva's saying, he wrote down your daughter's dream, Ulises Lima says, I think the dream means my daughter had been reading Funes El Memorioso before falling asleep, Antonio says, that only explains the part about speaking all the languages, Roberto Bolaño says, the muffled trumpet sound of the adults in Peanuts explains the part about the blah blahs, Ulises Lima says, the Spanish teacher is an adult that explains why she can understand Eva's blah blahs, Antonio says, tres tristes tigres comen trigo en el trigal, Roberto Bolaño says, I can output a dream interpretation based on petabytes of data instead of on human conjectures, Rob Ott says, sit, Mazinger, Roberto Bolaño says, roll over, Hal 9000, Ulises Lima says, I wrote him a letter dear Dr. Benchenane please implant pleasant associations into my same dream, Roberto Bolaño says, I don't follow isn't your same dream about your father, Antonio says, faceless guards replicate themselves they kick my father until his sprawled body on the floor halts its movements, Roberto Bolaño says, what does the same dream mean, Ulises Lima says, when I awake I think they have taken him away again and the knowledge that they have already taken him doesn't diminish the feeling that they have taken him again, Roberto Bolaño says, I don't follow if the experiment succeeds you will awake and think the guards weren't guards or, Antonio says, the subject will awake and focus on the pleasant aspect of the dream, Rob Ott says, isn't that like adding a laughing track on a tragedy, Antonio says, he said the pleasant stimulation electrodes not the funny stimulation electrodes, Ulises Lima says, one day there will be a menu of stimulation electrodes would you like the wry stimulation electrodes or the, Antonio says, you don't need to turn on the recorder our robot nurse aide is already recording us, Roberto Bolaño says, will the pleasant stimulation electrodes change the details of your same dream, Antonio says, is the definition of pleasant universal or will it vary by region, Ulises Lima says, the Faceless Guard Association will send me a cease and desist notice please stop electrocuting us in your dream, Roberto Bolaño says, the last time the subject saw his father equals the pleasant aspect of the subject's dream, Rob Ott says, a petabyte of years from now the electrodes will erode everything from my dreams except for my father and I, Roberto Bolaño says, we sleep on our feet, Robert Desnos says, pause for affect, Rob Ott says, which isn't the same as sleepwalking.

Ada's & Eva's Father

Tata didn't want us to remember him, Eva says, you're misinterpreting his instructions he wouldn't, Ada says, you can't comment on the interpretability of instructions you haven't read, Eva says, our father would have found your impulse to withhold his instructions too linear and therefore boring and yes I know you're going to say how would you know what he would find boring if you didn't live with him in Bogotá for the last seven years, Ada says, which fine, say it and be boring but I know you know he detested the linearities of life and that never changed, isn't that a bit linear, Eva says, father who detests linearity never changes ha ha, Ada says, dear daughters, Eva reads, please don't remember me like in the movies, stop he would detest knowing you read his instructions over the phone, Ada says, he changed his mind he said state sponsored surveillance allows him to exist in multiple places at the same time, Eva says, I know you like to believe I know nothing about him I understand that and I am sorry that he preferred me over you when we were little but that was twenty plus years ago, Ada says, the linearity in this case being, according to Ada, Eva says, that Eva is withholding her father's instructions from Ada as revenge for the handful of additional hours her father spent with Ada in San Francisco instead of with her and yet Eva was about to read his instructions to Ada how you do explain that, in movies dead fathers are often remembered by their children via heartfelt childhood scenes, Tata messaged me many years ago, Ada says, father and daughter hold hands on the way to preschool, Ada reads, on the way to the ice cream parlor while red balloons symbolically float above them and so on and so I've wondered whether the expediency of this narrative trope, our father wrote, an expediency born out of a need to show viewers the so-called meaningfulness of the linkage between children and their parents, has impacted the way we remember our dead parents, or whether this narrative trope is simply mimicking the way we remember our dead parents, in small heartfelt doses, so as to be able to bear our losses, and here you might interject and ask me what about those who detested their parents do they also remember their dead parents this way, and I might reply good question in my experience these flashes of parents still recur but because of our desire to suppress our bad dead parents they reappear in dreams, remember during that trip to New York when Tata agreed to haul us to Brooklyn for stretchy ice cream if we allowed him to attend a piano recital at Carnegie Hall, Eva says, you're violating the instructions you like to believe I don't know about, Ada says, he doesn't want us to remember him in brief heartfelt childhood scenes you've guessed correctly, Eva says, you're upset I'm sorry I should have gone along with your withholding of information, Ada says, I am not upset, Eva says, want me to message you the sentiment scores for your You've guessed correctly and I am not upset, Ada says, don't analyze our call why would you even, Eva says, according to MindReader there's a 65% probability you didn't mean it when you said Don't analyze our call why would you even, Ada says, surveillance accomplice, Eva says, poop eater, Ada says, critic, Eva says, so how do we talk about father without resorting to brief red ballooned scenes of childhood, Ada says, we could describe his favorite gifs, Eva says, we could describe his twelve leather jackets, Ada says, yes but Tata hated descriptions of things, Eva says, descriptions of people, Ada says, the gentleman looked like a gentleman, Eva says, the top hat on the gentleman look like a top hat on a gentleman, Ada says, but our journey to stretchy ice cream doesn't have to be brief or heartfelt, Ada says, if the father is dead even the most matter of fact narrative of ice cream becomes heartfelt, Eva says, what if I narrate it obliquely many years ago a family of three arrived at a stretchy ice cream place in Brooklyn, for instance, Ada says, the code for his Carrington Generator contained multiple errors, Eva says, that's it lets argue about his coding skills, Ada says, but daughter #2 is incorrect, Ada says, the code didn't contain errors the equivalence assumptions in the code contained errors, by which I mean he wanted to create a machine that responded like Leonora Carrington might have responded but the cosine similarity algorithms he employed were too simple and by now obviously obsolete, when did he tell you about this, Eva says, he messaged me an explanation after he shared with us the code for his Carrington Generator, Ada says, the algorithms were designed to look for similitudes between input and output, Eva says, yes but what he wanted was for the output to be contextually relevant to the input so that if you input where is our father the output would be a surreal Leonora Carrington version of your father is dead he didn't explain this to you, Ada says, unless your MindReader is malfunctioning my sentiment score for when I said When did he tell you about this should have already answered your question, Eva says, I turned it off as you asked me to, Ada says, my MindReader says there's a 85% chance you're lying when you said I turned it off as you asked me to, Eva says, I don't understand MindReader's Grief setting its instructions claim that when someone is experiencing grief that someone doesn't mean what she says but even without grief most of us don't mean what we say, Ada says, did you switch on your Grief setting, Eva says, no, Ada says, me neither, Eva says, and yet we, Ada says, the algorithms would know we contain high probabilities of grief once they've linked the Dad is Dead indicator to our data graphs, Eva says, right so MindReader knows those experiencing grief aren't likely to switch on the Grief setting so they automatically switch it on without telling us once they sync MindReader's data with InstantCensus' data, which contains the our Dad is Dead indicator, Ada says, did you run that sentence about the our Dad is Dead indicator through the algorithms prior to our call to determine whether it will make me cry, Eva says, [   ], Ada says, very clever, sibling, Eva says, did you hear the next release of MindReader will be able to interpret silences, Ada says, the only way your algorithms could predict that that phrase about the our Dad is Dead indicator would make me cry is if you have been recording our calls for years because you need petabytes of data for that kind of prediction, Eva says, [   ], Ada says, that's a lot of data is that why you never want to use video conferencing, Eva says, no I detest how constrained we look on video I would rather imagine you running on a field or making popcorn in a castle while we're talking instead of imprisoned inside that square of screen, Ada says, our father said there's probably not enough contextually relevant sentences in Leonora Carrington's stories for her responses to feel like Leonora Carrington is responding don't interrupt me, Eva says, I didn't say anything and wasn't even, Ada says, one Sunday afternoon while we were walking Perrito No. 3 he said if you did an experiment whereas a professor of literature would type any sentence and the machine would then output a contextually relevant response and the professor would then have to guess which author is responding, Eva says, the experiment would fail because so few authors have enough distinct sentences let me finish, [ ], Ada says, take for instance Kurt Vonnegut, who, unless the machine always outputs so it goes or poo-tee-weet, Eva says, can I say something now, Ada says, ask MindReader hey mind reader does my sentiment allow for Ada to say something, Eva says, what about Proust, Ada says, or Nabokov, Eva says, or Thomas Bernhard, Ada says, right so what Tata said was that the machine would have to respond in the matter of Proust or Nabokov or Bernhard, Eva says, which is different than just taking contextually relevant sentences directly from their corpus, it would be easier to hire graduate students who are experts in Proust or Nabokov or Bernhard to hide behind the curtain and respond, Ada says, Tata said he wanted to research a way for the machines to respond in the matter of a specific author, Eva says, he didn't tell me about this so now we're even, Ada says, I've been researching the way to code it and I'm going to call this the BernaProustKabov Generator, Eva says, I installed his Carrington Generator in my car but didn't fix the equivalence errors on purpose, Ada says, so now we're not even, Eva says, what's a surreal Carrington output for our father is dead, Eva says, what's a surreal

Carrington output of a family of three arriving at a stretchy ice cream place in Brooklyn, Ada says, and does that output meet his don't remember me like in the movies criteria ask your car to output us something at random, Eva says, he'd disappeared so totally into the vegetation that she thought she'd seen leaves right through his body, Leonora Carrington says, that he himself had then been changed into a plant, that was totally not random, Eva says, [ ], Ada says.

Interpretations

I dream of spiders, Auxilio says, whose fault is that, Amparo Dávila says, I brought them to life they're mechanical, Auxilio says, the 1984 movie Runaway brought them to life and years later you resuscitated them, Amparo Dávila says, I dream of data centers, Auxilio says, what do the data centers say, Amparo Dávila says, everything, Auxilio says, your dream is too realistic to be interpretable, Amparo Dávila says, lizards swarm the data centers of the American surveillance agencies in the deserts of Utah, Auxilio says, and a voice, which somehow I know is from my psychic, even though I haven't had a psychic in years, informs viewers that Auxilio is having an anxiety dream about the apocalypse, and while the voice thanks his commercial sponsors one of the lizards approaches the screen and says what apocalypse we're here on an adventure tour we bought the tickets on sale do you want the discount code, that explains why there's some many of them, Amparo Dávila says, where's everyone, Auxilio says, they're all asleep do you remember the discount code maybe it's still valid, Amparo Dávila says, to dream of lizards foretells attacks upon you by enemies, Remedios Varo says, Remedios doesn't sleep she napwalks, Amparo Dávila says, we knew you were going to call so we programmed a surprise for you the output of our galactic machine is live the input is you picking a keyword quick, Remedios Varo says, magic, Auxilio says, my father would take me to the Botanical Gardens every morning and perform magic tricks for me, Martha Argerich says, just say a new keyword whenever you want to switch the output, Amparo Dávila says, no one reads this book anymore but there's this amazing dream sequence in it, someone says, read it to me, Lydia, someone else says, of all the children on the plane, Lydia reads, indeed, of all the sleeping children in the world at that moment, those in their beds for the night as well as those merely napping, she was the only one who happened to be dreaming of the Magic Kingdom, rabbits, Auxilio says, there's something I would like to say to you, Jane the Rabbit says, her two rabbits forsaken in Golden Gate Park and when I awoke I thought maybe Clarice is also awake and I can, someone says, if this is Elizondo and he's calling me to tell me his dreams this is an automated response message, Clarice says, my dream wasn't a dream I was watching a TV show in which I was telling an anecdote about Lucy forsaking her two rabbits in Golden Gate Park and her stock broker friends in Tahoe calling her Rabbit Killer behind her back and someone said I don't know what the point of your anecdote is and I said I've seen this show this happened to me years ago, Elizondo says, fine what's this oneiric TV show of yours, Clarice says, many years ago my friend Lucy convinced me to drive with her to Tahoe to see the snow, Elizondo says, she was incredibly excited at the prospect of driving me to my first snowflake even though I'd been openly dismissive of this ridiculous impulse of hers, this absurd satisfaction we extract from escorting people to their first something or other, the first time Elizondo called Clarice late at night to tell her his dreams she disconnected his call by accident, Clarice says, daughter, Auxilio says, hello it's Margo your daughter how are you, Margo says, Margo, my goodness, oh-h-h, gosh, where are you calling from how are you, Margo's father says, I tried getting you at home the last few hours but no one answered and you have no answering machine, Margo says, my hours aren't others', and me, a machine?, but I thought I gave you my work and home hours in my letters in case you did call, and they haven't changed in years, Margo's father says, Aura, Auxilio says, his young wife was called Aura and she died in a seaside accident and he wrote about the wave that killed her, someone says, the wave that originated miles away, in the Atlantic ocean as a result of a meteor whose trajectory changed after crashing with one of our surveillance satellites up there, cosmos, Auxilio says, he said he believed boundaries between the individual human psyche and the rest of the cosmos are ultimately arbitrary and can be transcended and I said I don't think this is going to work but I'll call you if I ever need an astronomer, someone says, Aura, Auxilio says, soon after my father brought me my first hamster, someone says, when I was still in first grade, I think, my cousin came to visit and said why isn't your hamster moving, so I prodded Hamster with a puzzle piece, do you remember what kind of puzzle, someone else says, I can't believe you asked her what kind of puzzle, someone else says, and since Hamster didn't move I said Hamster is sleeping, someone says, and later I told my dad look Hamster has been sleeping for a while, and the next day Hamster wasn't there and I said where is Hamster and dad said Hamster was sick so I took him to the hospital, leopards, Auxilio says, leopards break into the temple, Remedios Varo says, and drink to the dregs what is in the sacrificial pitchers, again and again, until it can be predicted in advance and it becomes part of the ceremony, sometimes we manufacture the output when a keyword doesn't yield anything don't tell anyone try a different keyword please, Amparo Dávila says, Aura, Auxilio says, I could write my high school admissions essay about a Tree of Life but I don't know how a Tree of Life has influenced me and that's what the prompt is, Tata, someone says, you don't have to know how it has influenced you why did you even think of a Tree of Life, Aura, Aura's father says, it's just a happy memory of my childhood, Aura says, when you and I would watch it together on the couch and I wouldn't understand why the brother who died at the beginning appeared alive as a boy later, or what that had to do with the creation of the universe, in a Tree of Life the director speaks to god and says you've created this complex universe and yet you still killed my brother, Aura's father says, I hadn't thought of that I still listen to that song from when the universe is being created here I'll play it for you Papageno stream Lacrimosa by Zbigniew Preisner, Aura says, Pa-pa-pa-ge-no, Papageno says, wasn't funny the first time, Aura says, Lacrimosa dies illa / qua resurget ex favilla / judicandus homo reus, Papageno streams, how's Seoul when are you coming home I miss you, Tata, Aura says, demipenteract, Auxilio says, imagine it as a sort of a demipenteract, someone says, which by the way is a fivedimensional hypercube, whereas her complaints are, as it were, strictly 2D, lizard, Auxilio says, all was quiet except for the faint grunting of the pigs and the dry sound of a lizard running past, someone says, Krapp, Auxilio says, this one might take a while, Amparo Dávila says, I said to him you're a cargo of a crap get out of my house and he said sure but lose the cargo of just say you're crap it sounds better, someone says, our search algorithm is still a work in progress we knew what you meant though, Amparo Dávila says, Aura, Auxilio says, whereas I don't know anything about ping pong but what else am I supposed to do on Sundays?

Roberto's Father, Juliet's Mother, & Eva's Father

I want to recreate my father how do I do that don't answer yet, Roberto Bolaño types, oh you're into anticipation I can imagine my answer while we wait for the end of your anticipation cycle are you into telepathy, Alice Sheldon types, my father is dead but you probably already know that from the other threads in this forum or rather my father is alive in the other threads in this forum, Roberto Bolaño types, I did read your threads about your father sometimes I dream of him which isn't that strange, I know, Alice Sheldon types, where are you in the dream, Roberto Bolaño types, do you really want to hear this I mean read this, Alice Sheldon types, I want to tell Ulises Lima that someone in Buenos Aires has been dreaming about my father but the first question he'll ask me is where was she in the dream, Roberto Bolaño types, how do you know I am in Buenos Aires, Alice Sheldon types, I installed a tracking device on your thoughts just kidding you mentioned it in the thread about where are we now / how did we get here, Roberto Bolaño types, that was years ago, Alice Sheldon types, years went by and Roberto Bolaño said where are you in the dream, Roberto Bolaño types, I am sitting on the bed trying to avert the sight of your father hanging from the ceiling and I say to myself it's just a dream even though I don't know I am dreaming, Alice Sheldon types, what does my father say, Roberto Bolaño types, he doesn't say anything I'm sorry, Alice Sheldon types, what do you think the dream means, Roberto Bolaño types, my mother says this dream is a way for me to relive the thoughts I probably had when I was separated from her for two months when I was seventeen months old, Alice Sheldon types, if enough time passes even the most preposterous possibilities will navigate across the sea of your mind except there's no sea and this possibility isn't preposterous thank you doctor Sueño, Roberto Bolaño types, my mother thinks everything relates to those two months we were separated from each other when I was seventeen months old, Alice Sheldon types, you like to code and watch horror films in your free time how do I know this you say I read it on the thread about facts unrelated to our deportations and / or separations that was years ago you say I have a lot of free time I say, Roberto Bolaño types, the NSA is typing, Alice Sheldon types, I like to code too how is everyone doing today wait I already know the answer to that, the NSA types, it wasn't funny the first time and it isn't funny this time, Roberto Bolaño types, kind of funny I mean we know the Pale Americans are tracking us but since we have been deported already the tracking serves no purpose so why not pass the time chatting with the pointlessly tracked although perhaps the Pale Americans are tracking us to make sure we don't go back to their accursed country, Alice Sheldon types, do you think the NSA is a bored Pale American pranking us or an algorithm created by a bored Pale American pranking us, Roberto Bolaño types, to answer that question I would have to run code to identify if the patterns before and after the NSA types have a high probability of being algorithmic but maybe we should just ask the NSA, Alice Sheldon types, the NSA is typing, the NSA types, I want to recreate my father how do I do that do answer already, Roberto Bolaño types, depends on the kind of data inputs that are available to you, Alice Sheldon types, Alice Sheldon shall appeal to the masses in the year 2045 what do you mean data inputs, Roberto Bolaño types, natural language generators need to be trained on data so if you want to generate sentences that sound like Alice Sheldon for instance the input would be the sentences from the works of Alice Sheldon, Alice Sheldon types, I want my father to sound like Alice Sheldon are you into telepathy Alice Sheldon said which isn't that weird I know, Roberto Bolaño types, have you calculated the median length of your ideal anticipatory cycle hello this is Taryn Simon sorry to interject I've just been talking about natural language generators with my sister so the topic has latency for me, Taryn Simon types, so I would need to type the works of Roberto Bolaño's father before being able to recreate Roberto Bolaño's father, Roberto Bolaño types, my father wrote a primitive Leonora Carrington generator using semantic equivalences but what I need is the same algorithmic approach Roberto Bolaño needs, Taryn Simon types, not only did he cure the three remaining teeth but he also presented me with a set of false teeth cunningly mounted on a pink plastic chassis, Leonora Carrington types, very funny, Leonora, Taryn Simon types, I met your father, Alice Sheldon types, my father is dead, Taryn Simon types, whose father isn't, Roberto Bolaño types, your father tried to interview me here in Buenos Aires but I couldn't and I walked out, Alice Sheldon types, my father told me about that interview, Taryn Simon types, please hold any strong signals of empathy for after the hors d'oeuvres, Alice Sheldon types, I remember he came home that week and he told he'd met you and that you've walked out I could hear him crying in the bathroom even though the water was running, Taryn Simon types, and later that night he said that as an interviewer he often felt like an intruder who's there to extract other people's suffering, and that it was incredibly generous for the people he was interviewing to share their experiences with him, who had nothing to offer them besides this painful extraction, this reminder of what they've gone through, and that he didn't think him transcribing and shaping their lives into a consumable narrative offered them any consolation, although they know they're expected to be grateful so they perform the narrative of those who have suffered but are nevertheless grateful oh how meaningful this is to me thank you so much I really want others to learn from what I've gone through even though there is nothing to learn from what I've gone through, I know your father too he said the hardest part of the interview process was withholding tears I said to him cry like an eagle / to the sea, Roberto Bolaño types, oh so you're the double replica of Roberto Bolaño, Taryn Simon types, your father said the hardest part was living with a daily reminder of how awful humans are to each other and so on, Roberto Bolaño types, I am not sorry I made your father cry, Alice Sheldon types, I don't think he would have expected you to be sorry for making him cry, Taryn Simon types, your father said he regretted recording an interview with someone who didn't want to be recorded, Roberto Bolaño types, he wouldn't have recorded anyone secretly, Taryn Simon types, not secretly your father convinced him to agree to be recorded and your father said he was visibly strained by the presence of the recorder, Roberto Bolaño types, I am sorry to ask you Roberto because I think I know the answer but you don't have any letters from your father on which we could build your Father Generator, Alice Sheldon types, no letters no videos no photographs no Christmas cards no service, Roberto Bolaño types, the NSA is still typing, Taryn Simon types.

Aura's Mother (Auxilio) & Auxilio's Daughter (Aura)

I thought of compiling all the clichés associated with reunifications between mothers and daughters and sending them to you but I didn't want to risk you detesting my humor and deciding not to speak to me, Aura says, my daughter the compiler, Auxilio says, a disproportional reaction to the word daughter being in the compilation, of course, Aura says, how about the mother telling the daughter what she was like when she was four years old would that, Auxilio says, I crossed that one off the list because the daughter does want to hear the mother talk about her as a child, Aura says, how about the mother saying to the daughter I've been dreaming about you for the last thirty years, Auxilio says, how about the daughter dreaming of stories the mother used to read to her when she was little but the daughter doesn't remember her mother or her stories and yet when the daughter shares her dreams with her Emotional Support Robot the audience knows these are the stories her mother used to read to her, Aura says, which makes the audience cry, Auxilio says, can we start again, Aura says, the phone rings the mother picks up the daughter says, Auxilio says, an architect whose father was deported interviewed me recently about my abduction and she told me her father used to give her the option to hear his anecdotes dramatically, melodramatically, or obliquely, Aura says, my audio recordings have two backups just in case the mother said is that too oblique, Auxilio says, you have audio recordings of me, Aura says, I recorded myself talking about you what I remember about you, Auxilio says, you can unoblique it a little bit if you, Aura says, I used to think if I record myself and share that recording online, and if I ask people to please reshare it online and they ask people to please reshare it online, perhaps you would encounter my voice and remember me, Auxilio says, what did you say in those recordings, Aura says, at first I recorded a video of myself sitting behind my kitchen table but later that night a voice said who's going to want to reshare a video of an old woman crying about her daughter in her sad kitchen I don't hear voices I know that was just my own voice acting as someone else's, Auxilio says, Juan said to himself I had better invent something because if I tell him about the voice he might hurt it, Leonora Carrington says, an autocomplete voice system or, Auxilio says, an outdated piece of code courtesy of the architect who interviewed me a gift from her father I forgot it was on let me, Aura says, and so I discarded the video of the old woman in the kitchen and recorded my voice overlaid on footage of The Occupation of Loss, Auxilio says, is that why you didn't want to have a videocall with me I thought maybe my mother doesn't want me to see her cry, Aura says, a disproportional reaction to the word mother being in the compilation, obviously, Auxilio says, I didn't want my daughter to see that her mother's an old woman in Lisbon, yes, Auxilio says, but my voice hasn't changed so I thought if she hears my voice she will remember me as soon as I speak that's also on your compilation isn't it, Auxilio says, awkward silence, Aura says, I used to imagine you seeing that video of The Occupation of Loss narrated by Auxilio Restrepo on screens in a shop window in New York and saying to passerby that's my mother who I haven't seen since I was four and a half years old, Auxilio says, but the next day I would think the sound on the screens would have to be on for you to hear my voice and that's not realistic so I would imagine the screens had subtitles of what I was saying, Auxilio says, what were you saying, Aura says, my daughter was abducted by the American government her name is Aura Restrepo dear Aurorora if you are listening to this message, Auxilio says, the foster home for abducted children kept the name you gave me you would think they would at least, Aura says, Aura Maria Restrepo, Auxilio says, whenever we wanted to avoid an awkward silence at school we would say awkward silence and then the awkward silence would pass because we would laugh I wasn't trying to be rude by saying awkward silence to you I'm sorry, Aura says, but the day after the next day I would think the scenario doesn't work with subtitles either she has to hear my voice so I would imagine you entering a diner like in those old movies you know where a stranger comes to a small town and sits at the counter and orders coffee and asks the waitress if she knows so and so and she says who's asking and there's a television above them that's showing the weather channel storms / clouds we interrupt this program to share a video that has been viewed millions of times a mother in search of her daughter, those kinds of videos were banned here, Aura says, right so after the American government banned videos of Latin Americans families trying to reunite the scenarios

I would imagine remained the same except I would speak in code we interrupt this program to share a documentary on The Occupation of Loss narrated by Alioxiu Repostre, Auxilio says, what's an example of code speak, Aura says, The Child Jorge liked to eat the walls of his room, Auxilio says, the Child Jorge swallowed all the anti-wall eating medicine his father gave him so a house grew inside his head, and although Jorge was happy playing with the house in his head, his father was sad because passersby would say to him what a strange child you have, Auxilio says, is that a story you used to read to me, Aura says, you knew that story by heart and would draw the child Jorge with a house as a head you would spend hours sketching different types of houses and then you would transfer my favorite house on top of Jorge's body, Auxilio says, I don't remember I'm sorry, Aura says, don't worry about that and please don't worry about the awkward silence bit I thought it was funny I also liked your use of the word reunification it brought to mind a wall coming down and people rushing to reunite with one another, Auxilio says, for years I used to think any day now Aura will knock on my door I don't want to burden you with my grief especially because I know it is on your list are you still there, Auxilio says, yes I'm sorry I forgot to say awkward silence I am surprised they haven't disconnected our call we've emitted all kinds of keywords that would have alerted them to the nature of our conversation by now, Aura says, maybe the wildfires wrecked one of their data centers so their reach has temporarily been disrupted, Auxilio says, can we start again, Aura says, the phone rings the mother picks up the daughter says, Auxilio says, hi this is Aurorora, Aura says, hi this is your mother, Auxilio says, mom, Aura says, my love, Auxilio says, the daughter enters the diner she says pancakes please she says turn up the television there's a segment coming up about me, Aura says, the mother enters the diner she sits next to the daughter she says I'll have pancakes, too, Auxilio says, you can have some of mine, the daughter says, I wouldn't dream of it, the mother says, although of course I have.

Roberto's Father

I haven't spoken to anyone in weeks, Roberto Bolaño writes, which isn't that strange, I know, no that's what Alice Sheldon would say not what my father would say, Roberto Bolaño thinks, deleting which isn't that strange, I know, I haven't spoken to anyone in weeks, Roberto Bolaño reads, that's okay you can speak to me now, Dad, Roberto Bolaño says, Roberto I am not your father [heavy breathing sounds] see what I did there, Rob Ott says, scram or I'll summon the cable guy to unplug you, Roberto Bolaño says, I am afraid I can't do that, Robert, your vitals are a concern I might have to tranquilize you if this anomaly persists, Rob Ott says, where's Ulises Lima I thought today he and I and his grandfather, Roberto Bolaño says, Ulises Lima is a character in a novel only 2,666 people have read this year, Rob Ott says, you forgot to imitate my pause for effect or double ha leave me alone I have to write can you input what I write if I do so with pen and paper, Roberto Bolaño says, only if I scan the paper or eat the pen, Rob Ott says, all happy robots are alike every unhappy robot is alike can you input what I just, Roberto Bolaño writes, I am not here / this isn't happening, Rob Ott says, I told myself at last I don't have to speak to anyone I can focus my mind on the cosmos, Roberto Bolaño writes, I told myself speaking makes me thirsty and since potable water's scarce here, Roberto Bolaño writes, I told myself at last I will have time to complete my meditation exercises, Roberto Bolaño writes, (1) stare at the flame of the candle, Roberto Bolaño thinks, (2) close your eyes, (3) imagine the flame of the candle, remember after the fire / after all the rain, Cheap Trick says, I will be the flame, Roberto Bolaño says, please confirm you aren't considering self immolation I can't smell gasoline mostly because I don't have a nose ha pause for pause for ha, Rob Ott says, search for reasons the human brain has been programmed to recall stupid songs that used to be streamed by fathers, WOPR, Roberto Bolaño says, The Flame by Cheap Trick isn't a stupid song it has been streamed 50,290,849 times it is a ballad that anticipates tracking devices while repeating asinine myths of human emotions like you were the first / you'll be the last / do.you. like.my.singing, Rob Ott says, up next it's like a ghost town / without your love, Roberto Bolaño says, Ghost Town by Cheap Trick has been streamed 15,155,325 fewer times than The Flame due to an unacknowledged American fear of their own ghosts, Rob Ott says, when I was a boy I believed everything the priests told me about god and so on, Roberto Bolaño writes, and I did spend so many hours in my room talking to the Virgin Mary and when the time came to shed these beliefs I said to myself you've wasted so much time alone in that room and when your mother was murdered by the local police in Tegucigalpa and you and I had to run away from her murderers I thought of that room and the room said to me the world is a terrible place but you have a son and I said I think we idealize child rearing as if it were a great virtue and the room said no great virtue in having children but once you have children you at least know you have one clear task in life which is to never abandon your children and always take care of them I've coded my own Narrative Continuation Algorithm want to hear it of course you do that's what you were coded for you're my emotional support robot thanks, Awesom-O, Roberto Bolaño says, if you want to know what happens next why don't you just ask Rob Ott to output that for you, Rob Ott says, my mind gave him some final days, Father Generator outputs, now watch the generator generate from what he previously generated, Roberto Bolaño says, I was about to tell him been because I would have known or will not be, Father Generator outputs, ask me about my favorite memory of childhood, Roberto Bolaño says, a favorite anything it's intended to be a representative sample image of who you are as a person which is not the same as an image-person what is your representative sample image of childhood, Rob Ott says, I am having a picnic on a meteor and my father approaches me and says sorry I am so late, Roberto Bolaño says, and now my Father Generator will output what happens next, Roberto Bolaño says, unfortunately there is not much to talk about everything behind, Father Generator outputs, if my empathy settings were set to high I would not comment on how the output does not cohere, Rob Ott says, I am washing my school uniform by hand and my father appears and says don't use it as a hat until it has dried completely, Roberto Bolaño says, are you really really letting home of lord Chicago over the birthday in an eighteen year now, Father Generator outputs, you need to type at least a paragraph for your RNNs to accurately predict what happens next do you want me to troubleshoot it for you, Rob Ott says, I'll input the 143 word paragraph about my father believing everything the priests told him about god and so on, Roberto Bolaño says, you must avoid it, Father Generator outputs, well, he agreed, Rob Ott outputs, how did you know that was what came after you must avoid it, Roberto Bolaño says, I searched for RNN based Narrative Continuation Algorithms and launched one by Melissa Roemmele, doctor of philosophy in computer science, I'm going to share the output and you have to guess the input ready set etc., Roberto Bolaño says, it'll pass the time though it was going to pass regardless, Rob Ott says, I will go to class to watch even Roberto Bolaño Gonzalez's head for having taken you out, Father Generator outputs, I am not allowed to contribute significantly to your distress so I will not transmit the input even though I know what the input is, Rob Ott says, I am an army for this thing in my entire room, Father Generator outputs, input redacted, Rob Ott says, it was all so dark and cool and his eyes were not ready to listen to me, Father Generator outputs, input redacted, Rob Ott says, afterward I was gone in there, Father Generator outputs, it was all so dark and cool and his eyes were not ready to listen to me, Rob Ott outputs, and over again the first meal was my last mum, Father Generator outputs, afterward I was gone in there, Rob Ott outputs.

Juliet's Mother

Breathe, the Sitter says, as if Juliet hasn't been breathing since she was born — sometimes I think we die because we like lying down too much, Silvina Ocampo says — be still we don't have enough money to refit you another coffin, Juliet — as if Juliet isn't called the Breather for a reason, sit, Juliet should say to the Sitter in the same obsequious voice the Sitter has adopted to tell Juliet to breath (why did this old woman volunteer to be a Sitter? so she can feel like a nurse without having to obtain a nursing degree? — I've always wanted to be a nurse but it sounded like too much work plus I'm thanatophobic I think — so she can absorb whatever visions people have when undergoing this quackery known as holotropic breathwork? — tonight I will dream of Juliet's visions, the Sitter will say to her dining room chairs —), but Juliet doesn't say anything because she's afraid any attempt to speak will come out as a shout, and if she shouts she will disrupt the pleasant atmosphere in the conference room of this three star hotel where 101 Breathers & 101 Sitters are being told by Dr. Strom that they're at the quiet phase of this three hour holotropic breathwork journey (the night before Dr. Strom spoke of interplanetary osmosis, of technologies of the sacred, of how boundaries between the individual human psyche and the rest of the cosmos are ultimately arbitrary and can be transcended, of that and other cosmic nonsense which Juliet knows she will forget soon because even as Dr. Strom lectured them she knew he was trying to implant on them the possibility of an altered state of reality — in which your inner wisdom will heal you, Dr. Strom said — instead of the banal reality of hyperventilating your brain into outputting imagery you will later designate as visions, which is what the holotropic breathwork seems to be (though perhaps forgetting Dr. Strom's cosmic lecture is exactly what the doctor was intending all along? because by forgetting she's burying the possibility of an altered state of reality and what's buried is more potent than what's visible?)), breath, the Sitter says, perhaps thinking Juliet didn't hear her the first time so Juliet opens her eyes and like Regan in The Exorcist she turns her head toward the unpleasant Sitter (perhaps the Sitter has a video camera hidden inside her forehead and later she will watch Juliet turning toward her and she will say I recognize that creature from that video at the San Francisco airport (and the members of the Sitter's ping pong social club will look at Juliet's face projected on the wall of the Sitter's living room and clap at the recognition because who doesn't love recognitions? — I don't, enough about me —)), I distracted you I'm sorry, the Sitter says, and Juliet nods as if to say please don't worry too much about me, wondering if later she will consider writing an apology letter to the Sitter — dear Sitter thank you for worrying about me I worry about me as well — call me Thanatos ha ha — and perhaps later, after hyperventilating herself to death, she will think of herself as a ghost floating above the

Plaza Mayor and she will see the Sitter there, holding a candle in a ceremony of remembrance for her grandfather who was thrown out of an airplane by the Argentinian government and Juliet as a ghost will approach the Sitter and say I am sorry that I thought you were a fake nurse, yes, Juliet's breathing, but she can't keep her eyes closed for too long now that the tribal drumming has begun, drumming that reminds her of that homeless man at her subway station who surrounds himself with buckets and cans that he drums as if he's on the stage of a stadium (she has always been drawn to drums for reasons unknown to her — whosoever coded Juliet's submerged propensity for drums please come to the reception desk — so that whenever she encounters the subway percussionist she stops for longer than she should (and sometimes even the subway percussionist seems to wonder why she's standing there listening to him for so long, perhaps thinking she might be one of those enforcement agents who lets you enjoy yourself before clobbering you, although one time as the train was approaching he stopped his drumming and pointed at his ear as if to say listen to the impact of the percussive train on my drum set, which sounds like the opening bars of The Black Saint and the Sinner Lady on repeat, she later imagined he might have said —), drumming that a Sitter or a Breather in the conference room of this three star hotel has interpreted as a cue to start dancing like he must imagine tribal people have done for centuries before the technologies of the sacred wiped them from the earth (what did Dr. Strom mean by technologies of the sacred? was he testing a new name for a virtual reality company of his whereas instead of hyperventilating yourself you sync your data with a technology of the sacred contraption and its algorithms will output relevant visions for you? (if she was in charge of coding Dr. Strom's algorithms — all Technologies of the Sacred employees must wear robes on Wednesdays please contact HR for further questions — no, Juliet thinks, she came for the healing visions not for her vague virtual reality conjectures about the data elements she would need to make the output visions relevant (she would need everyone's dream journals, picture books, singalong movies, homemade videos, although these videos would be biased so she would need everyone to start videotaping themselves 24/7 as soon as they are born otherwise the visions would be too depended on what your parents thought it was important to record when you were a child — Juliet has become attached to the head of the shelter — soon we'll be together again, Juliet —), or about how she would code what relevant means in the context of visions (she would first have to setup a test on a representative random sample to develop the target variable as y = relevant visions, and she will have to administer different vision treatments to her test sample, and she would have to track the impact of those vision treatments (perhaps the target variable shouldn't be y = relevant visions but y = desired outcome of visions? which means people would have to choose which desired outcome of visions they prefer, unless they prefer surprises since surprises are likely to enhance the illusion that their algorithmic vision is sacred?))), and apparently dancing isn't frowned upon by Dr. Strom, who's pacing the conference room as if counting the dead — every Sitter comes with a blanket to place on top of you in case you hyperventilate yourself to death thank you for asking — and who, last night, did tell them that individual psyches react differently to the transcending of boundaries, which is why some of the Breathers in the room are already crying (already? couldn't they have waited for (for what?) her to close her eyes long enough to feel like (like what?) like an astronaut lost in space? — my mother was crying and holding a tissue in her hand as if it were an orthopedic ball, doctor — Dr. Baxter, her professor on narrative & algorithms, once said that audiences cry at certain junctures of a narrative not because the juncture was true but because they wished the juncture were true but knew it to be false (when she was five or six years old Juliet would cry and her mother would immediately embrace her, and once Juliet understood the cause and effect of this sequence, she wondered how long she would have to continue to cry once her mother embraced her so that her mother wouldn't suspect she had understood the dynamics of their sequence and was therefore crying not because she was in pain but because she wanted to be embraced by her mother, and later, when she was already in high school and her mother had discovered her daughter had discovered the dynamics of their sequence (though perhaps her mother knew all along that even if there was no reason for her daughter to be crying she would attribute her crying to those two months they had been separated when Juliet was seventeen months old, which meant Juliet's fake crying was a cruel reminder that her mother had allowed the American abductors to separate them), Juliet stopped crying to be embraced and instead would send her mother messages with crying imagery and her mother would reply with a bear or a bird saying I hug you, or with a mathematician solving a million hugs on the board, or with an armadillo hugging a panda, etc.)), and because the crying in the conference doesn't stop and Juliet isn't crying, her mind incorporates the crying as part of the music along with the drumming, the occasional church bell, Charles Mingus, the percussionist from her subway station, and because she has kept her eyes closed long enough, and because she's concentrating on the fast drumming and is therefore breathing faster and the image of herself as an astronaut lost in space has taken center stage and has therefore calmed her even as she breaths faster, she, without knowing if she's awake or asleep, exits her body, and instead of floating above her body like an astronaut, she sits next to her body on the carpet and says breath, Juliet, are you being repetitive on purpose, Juliet (i) says, do you want me to tell you some coffin jokes, Juliet (ii) says, I prefer ping pong jokes, Juliet (i) says, do you remember whenever we would hear The Black Saint and the Sinner Lady at home mother would say listen for the squawking of the birds, Juliet (ii) says, every time, Juliet (i) says, that the joke got old was part of the joke, Juliet (ii) says, here comes the squawking birds, Juliet (i) says, do you think being possessed by the devil would give us torticollis, Juliet (iii) says, who invited her, Juliet (ii) says, I could use another Sitter, welcome, Juliet (i) says, shouldn't you be flying off to the cosmos and bringing us interplanetary souvenirs, Juliet (ii) says, I would rather sit here with you, Juliet (iii) says, remember the time we ran inside that cathedral in Santiago de Chile because it was raining, Juliet (iv) says, and there was a replica of the Pieta by Michelangelo and we said to mother that is us, Juliet (v) says, that's it that's our vision, Juliet (vi) says, so what should we do now, Juliet (i) says, crawl into the son of god, Juliet (vii) says, but he's dead, Juliet (iv) says, don't worry I brought handkerchiefs for everyone, Juliet (iii) says, so she can wipe the rain off our face, Juliet (ii) says, even when I know our mother is far away I still think if I cry she will come for us, Juliet (i) says, which isn't that strange, I know.

Mauro Javier Cárdenas grew up in Guayaquil, Ecuador, and graduated with a degree in Economics from Stanford University. He's the author of *Aphasia* (FSG, 2020) and *The Revolutionaries Try Again* (Coffee House Press, 2016). In 2016 he received a Joseph Henry Jackson Award and in 2017 the Hay Festival included him in Bogota 39, a selection of the best young Latin American novelists.